W9-BVU-023

Praise for *An Eternal Lei*

"A thrilling cozy with a gutsy young sleuth in authentic, contemporary Hawaii; packed with cultural insights and twisty reveals, it's paradise in a book."

—**Jennifer J. Chow**, Lefty Award-Nominated
author of the *Sassy Cat Mysteries*

"Kamaʻāina rejoice! Naomi Hirahara has served up a detective who looks, talks and acts like one of us, a true breath of fresh air. . . . *An Eternal Lei* is a cozy with a hardboiled heart, overflowing with Leilani's cynical observations and introspection and staring down one of the Pacific's ugliest issues without flinching. It's a rainbow shave ice complete with azuki beans and ice cream for those of us who like something dark and rich lurking under the pretty colors."

—**Scott Kikkawa**, Elliot Cades Award winning author
of *Kona Winds* and *Red Dirt*, and
associate editor of *The Hawaiʻi Review of Books*

An Eternal Lei

Also by Naomi Hirahara

Historical Mysteries
Clark and Division

Leilani Santiago Hawai'i Mysteries
Iced in Paradise

Officer Ellie Rush Mysteries
Murder on Bamboo Lane
Grave on Grand Avenue

Mas Arai Mysteries
Summer of the Big Bachi
Gasa-Gasa Girl
Snakeskin Shamisen
Blood Hina
Strawberry Yellow
Sayonara Slam
Hiroshima Boy

For Colleen

3 1526 05614456 8

An Eternal Lei

A Leilani Santiago Hawai'i Mystery

Naomi Hirahara

PROSPECT
· PARK ·
BOOKS

Prospect Park Books
an imprint of Turner Publishing Company
Nashville, Tennessee

www.turnerpublishing.com

An Eternal Lei

Copyright © 2022 by Naomi Hirahara. All rights reserved.

This book or any part thereof may not be reproduced or transmitted in any form
or by any means, electronic or mechanical, including photocopying, recording, or
by any information storage and retrieval system, without permission in writing
from the publisher.

This is a work of fiction. All the characters and events portrayed in this book are
either products of the author's imagination or are used fictitiously.

Cover art by Edwin Ushiro
Cover design by Susan Olinsky and Grace Cavalier
Book design by Tim Holtz

Library of Congress Cataloging-in-Publication Data
Names: Hirahara, Naomi, 1962- author.
Title: An eternal lei / by Naomi Hirahara.
Description: Nashville : Prospect Park Books, 2022. | Series: Leilani
    Santiago Hawai'i mystery
Identifiers: LCCN 2021025576 (print) | LCCN 2021025577 (ebook) | ISBN
    9781684427963 (paperback) | ISBN 9781684427970 (hardcover) | ISBN
    9781684427987 (ebook)
Subjects: GSAFD: Mystery fiction.
Classification: LCC PS3608.I76 E84 2022 (print) | LCC PS3608.I76 (ebook)
    | DDC 813/.6--dc23
LC record available at https://lccn.loc.gov/2021025576
LC ebook record available at https://lccn.loc.gov/2021025577

Printed in the United States of America

Chapter One

AT FIRST MY SISTER DANI thought she saw a giant jellyfish bobbing on the surface of Waimea Bay. The brown tentacles seemed to be floating from a tan hull. Dani was only nine at the time and an artist with an active imagination; that pandemic season she was constantly drawing menehune, Hawai'i's mythological troll people carrying water in buckets from the Waimea River.

In her defense, there were a lot of creatures appearing out of the ocean and sky in Kaua'i that year. Our visitors had decreased almost 74 percent. The lack of humans traipsing around our island, taking selfies, snorkeling, and leaving their plastic cups and straws signaled for nature to heal and flourish.

Dani, being Dani, wanted to commune with that giant jellyfish. She was unafraid of its potential sting, after which, when I was a kid, we'd do shi-shi on our legs to mitigate the pain. Her wavy golden hair was long then—well, all of our hair was long that year. I had attempted to shave my father's hair, but accidentally pushed too hard on the clippers. Aisus! A bald spot on the back of the head and a tuft of curls on our linoleum kitchen floor. I didn't bother to alert my father to my mishap and just arranged some longer curls over the empty space. Dad luckily wasn't the type to check the back of his head in a mirror, and no one he knew would dare to make an insulting remark about his personal appearance.

While Dani was approaching her target, our fifteen-year-old sister, Sophie, was on the beach, watching something on YouTube on her phone.

"Sophie," Dani screamed. "It's a lady!"

Together they were able to pull the woman's body onto the shore. Dani was the one who ran to Waimea Junction while Sophie, for once showing good judgment, dialed 911 and stayed behind.

Dani, soaking wet and the top half of her looking like a mermaid, breathed hard as she stood in the doorway of Lee's Leis and Flowers, where I was stringing leis with Mrs. Lee, my best friend's mother. "Leilani, there's a dead woman in the ocean!"

I dropped the orchid from my grasp and slipped off my Crocs. Normally I would have easily been able to outrun Dani; but because of the "pandemic fifteen" around my middle, I huffed and puffed more than usual. From the rock jetty, I spied the prostrate woman, who could have been mistaken for a tangle of seaweed on the shore. My bare feet kicked up wet sand as I neared the body.

The woman looked somewhat familiar, but then, she could have been any fortysomething kama'āina from Kaua'i in a low-cut one-piece swimsuit. She was Asian, or maybe part Polynesian, with dark, wavy hair. I stood there for a moment, not knowing what to do. "Is she breathing?" Sophie called out.

It was barely noticeable, but yes, she was breathing. I had learned CPR at my old work in Seattle. I knew what to do, but I couldn't move. We had been wearing masks for months and ordered to stay six feet away from people outside our household, so to put my lips on the lips of a stranger seemed not only awkward but also a death sentence. Dani had caught up with me. "You gonna help her, right, Leilani?"

Dammit, I had no choice.

The woman was wearing a lei, which I ripped off her body, revealing blisters all around her chest and back. Great. The woman looked diseased. I placed her face to one side, as I had been taught in my CPR class, and pushed on her small chest. Water flowed from her mouth, but she still remained unconscious. Like I said, she was breathing, but barely. Pinching her nose, I blew my air into her mouth around a half dozen times. Her chest hardly moved. I repeated the whole sequence, not knowing if I was making a difference, but not having the time to doubt.

I was almost ready to quit when the paramedics, dressed in white shirts and dark slacks, arrived with a gurney. "We got it," they said in muffled voices through their masks. I stepped aside, barely aware of the aid they were administering. I had gone to high school with one of them, Rocket Nakayama, also dripping wet. He raised his arm to me before they lifted the woman onto the gurney and trudged up the sand.

Sophie, carrying what looked like the woman's clothes, and Dani ran after them, but I stayed behind. In the rush of attempting to keep the woman alive, my adrenaline had kicked into gear, but now my anxiety was starting to overtake me. What was I thinking, giving this stranger mouth-to-mouth? There was no doubt that I had contracted the virus. I already felt short of breath, and my lungs ached.

I turned and saw the broken lei on the beach. I should have left it there. Let the sea swallow it into its depths. But maybe because I had spent so many weeks making leis and arrangements for my best friend Court Kahuakai's family business, Lee's Leis and Flowers, I couldn't just forget it. Someone, maybe even me, had spent time threading the flowers and selecting the perfect greens. These were not the typical purplish-pink orchid leis that airlines and hotels presented to tourists. Nestled amid this flower strand were greenish mokihana berries, Kaua'i's official plant material, which made my fingers smell a little like licorice after stringing them. They were rare and expensive, available only on our island. So out of respect for the mokihana and the arrangement's creator, I picked up that broken lei, carried it to our shave ice stand, dropped it in a plastic bag, and placed it in our refrigerator, next to a carton of ripe mangoes we were going to include in food giveaways. If I hadn't done that, I think everything would have turned out differently. The mokihana knew secrets that we were only starting to discover.

The next thing I did after storing the lei was to head for the bathroom. I was able to find a bottle of hydrogen peroxide. I gargled a couple of times with the clear liquid, spitting out any germs from the mystery woman. And then I thoroughly washed my fingers as if I were a doctor preparing for surgery.

By the time I emerged from our now-shuttered shave ice stand, a black and white car marked Kaua'i Police Department was parked out front in the Waimea Junction lot. Waimea Junction had been my second home since I was born. It was a cluster of storefronts: the originals—Lee's Leis and Flowers, our Santiago's Shave Ice, my father's Killer Wave surf and snorkel shop, and D-Man's corner watering hole—next to a new one, Books and Suds, our landlord's soap and used bookstore that never really got off the ground. My breathing grew shallow again and I got chicken skin, my typical reaction when I see the police. It was a visceral reaction from the times I was in the back seat of a squad car during my troubled teenage years.

Standing in the parking lot was only one police officer: Andy Mabalot, my high school classmate. He had recently announced his engagement to one of our former part-time workers, Sammie Nunes, who somehow had gotten through nursing school at Kaua'i Community College and now worked as a nurse at our local hospital. His engagement helped define our friendship, much to my relief. We were clearly buddies, no romance involved.

"Hey, howzit." Andy had on a black mask, similar to the ones the paramedics had worn. A line of sweat ran down the sides of his face. It was October, and the mayor had announced that the island had to prepare for another coronavirus surge. "I heard you did CPR on that woman on the beach. You should go to the hospital for a COVID test. Sammie's been working the line."

I nodded.

"Were you the one who found her?"

"Dani was. And then me." Sophie, as usual, seemed to come out of nowhere.

Dani walked slowly from the shave ice shack, biting the end of a plastic spoon. She was as suspicious as I was of the police, even though today it came in the shape of Andy.

Andy had Dani sit across from him on a picnic bench. "Tell me everyting that you saw."

"Huh?" Dani craned her ear toward Andy, not understanding what he was saying. He was the type who mumbled his words anyway, so the mask wasn't doing him any favors.

"Tell him what happened at the beach," I interpreted.

Dani recounted her story, giant jellyfish and all.

Sophie, not to be outdone by her younger sister, interrupted a few times. "Only able to pull her in because I went in to help."

"Had you seen this woman before?'

Both Dani and Sophie shook their wet heads.

"She not from Waimea," I added. That much I knew for sure.

Emily, the second of us four Santiago sisters, just a year younger than me, crossed the street wearing a maroon Santa Clara University mask, a backpack hanging from her right shoulder. From the time she began attending law school in California, her gait had changed. Before, she had sauntered, but now she almost marched, as if she'd been imbued with a new sense of purpose. "What happened?" she asked as she neared the picnic table.

"Em, it's so awful." Dani got up and wrapped her arms around Emily's shoulders. They were the two Santiago sisters with golden hair. They looked like fairy princesses—I mean real fairies from the wilderness. In a second, Sophie, dark-haired like me, was also part of the group hug.

For two weeks after disembarking from Southwest Airlines from San Jose last August to finish her law school studies from home, Emily had had to quarantine herself in my bedroom while all of us left meals for her by the door. Ever since she could leave that room, the girls had followed her every move.

Even Andy's face softened when he saw Emily and the girls in the tight embrace. He transformed into the old Andy, the Andy who had ordered super grape shave ice with two generous squirts of syrup. "Maybe we can take a little break." He turned his attention to me. "Can you do me a favor?"

I waited.

"Can I have a shave ice?"

Doing something mundane from life *before* was actually a relief. I ran a clean rag over our shave ice machine, which had been sitting there unused for months. We still kept the electricity on in our shop because we were storing a lot of perishables for a food bank that my landlord was running every two weeks. I had removed a lot of shave ice molds from the freezer to make room for whole chickens, but luckily I found one ice mold to use today.

Last year, business had been going gangbusters. I had even convinced Baachan, my grandma, to switch to a Square wireless payment system. She fought it tooth and nail; but when she discovered how simple it was—insert credit card and voila, instant sale—she was completely sold. She became so excited to make transactions that she was constantly bothering people, even our landlord, Sean, to buy anything—even a twenty-five-cent postcard—with a credit or debit card. I was considering maybe opening a pop-up store in California, specifically in Silicon Valley, where our Sean was from. Back then, there were no limits, and I was more than surprised to discover that I had gotten so into making the business a success.

Everything had changed this year. Baachan might have been affected the most. Despite her saltiness, she loved being in the thick of things, whether it be at the shave ice shack or at her ukulele lessons. All of that was gone now. Shōganai, she said. It can't be helped.

Sean waived our rent money. That saved our skin, for sure. Dad pivoted from producing his Killer Wave Hawaiian shirts to using his ridiculous fabric for making masks. Since inter-island travel was being allowed without a quarantine, he was in Oʻahu now, making his pitch to the ABC store chain. Mom was at the sewing machine making the prototypes, while Dani, the most artistic of all us Santiago sisters, pinned fabric and cut out patterns when she wasn't Zooming for school.

Killer Wave, my dad's surf shop, was now open by appointment only for locals who needed some surf wax or maybe a repair. Kelly Kahuakai, my longtime buddy, brief romantic interest (small kid stuff!), and Court's husband, left the shop to join his new bride's flower business next door, which was way more lucrative, anyway. Although we didn't have visitors coming to get married on the island, folks were still having intimate weddings, graduation and anniversary celebrations, and funerals. Kelly was also attempting to expand onto the Mainland with an online business. Pekelo, Kelly's brother, had moved out of the shed in the back of his and Kelly's family house—much to Court's relief—and found a job with a kalo farm in the Hanalei Valley on the North Shore. He had given up—for now—a return to the military, and instead of a gun he brandished a machete. He stayed primarily in a spare room of our family friend, Rick Chen, in Hanalei.

D-man, my surrogate father, had to close his outdoor bar in the Junction for a few months, but, due to a new ruling in June, had reopened and was even more popular than ever. I wanted to help D-man, but my father, now a recovering alcoholic and having a complicated relationship with the old surfer, banned me from being a bartender.

Everyone seemed to have a new purpose, but, to tell you the truth, I was lost. I had to say goodbye to my dreams of taking my shave ice concoctions to the rest of the world. I did sometimes say shōganai like Baachan, but, more often than not, I felt as mad as hell.

I tried to cope by making ices for everyone. I knew what everyone wanted without asking. Andy's super grape, Sophie's Blue Monster, which literally is a monster combination with blueberry and root beer (no chocolate ice cream today), Dani's passionfruit, and Emily's coconut. For myself, an ice with Kona coffee, black with no cream or sweetener.

We sat at the picnic table, probably only six inches apart. I know Mayor Kawakami would not have been happy that we weren't social-distancing, but at least we were sitting outside. Anyway, Emily, the girls, and I were part of the same household. It was only Andy who was the outsider, the person outside our safe pod.

The Lee's delivery vehicle, a red minivan, pulled into the parking lot. Court and Kelly, both wearing Killer Wave masks, emerged, Kelly first. Court was now literally waddling, her swollen belly resembling a giant mango.

"Look at the lady that we found in the ocean, Court!" Sophie ran up to her, holding out her phone as Court struggled toward the picnic table.

"Put on your mask." Kelly, who before had been all smiles and sunshine, had become ultra-protective during his evolution into a future father.

Leaving her phone with Court, Sophie ran inside the shack, while I pulled my mask up from around my neck.

Court, one hand on her belly, studied the photo on Sophie's phone. "I've seen this woman," she said.

Andy leapt from the picnic bench and slid on his mask, hiding his purple-stained lips. He was now sporting his sunglasses, making him look more imposing and less like 'ohana. He stepped a few feet closer to Court.

"She ordered a lei from me. A mokihana one."

"When was this?" Andy started typing on his phone.

"Yesterday late afternoon. She was my last customer. I told her that I couldn't get the mokihana berries until the next day."

"Did she pay with credit?"

"No, cash."

"Did she say anyting?"

"She seemed, well, a bit off. She couldn't get her words out right, rememba, Kelly?

Kelly was uncharacteristically quiet, frown lines over his big brown eyes.

Andy glanced at the eaves of Waimea Junction. "You have that new security system, eh?"

One of the improvements our landlord Sean made when he took over the building was to install some cameras throughout Waimea Junction. We'd had some petty burglaries over the past few years, and he figured that it would at least be a deterrent.

"That equipment's jacked up," Kelly said.

"I haven't heard of any problems with it." Court readjusted her mask so it sat higher on her nose.

I sensed some domestic discord and butted in. "Anyway, you have to talk to Sean about all dat."

Sophie, wearing her Harley Quinn mask, emerged holding something in her skinny right hand.

"Hey, Leilani, is this the lei that the lady was wearing? Found it in the refrigerator."

I couldn't see Andy's eyes through his sunglasses, but I could figure out what he was thinking. *Leilani Santiago is holding out on the police again.*

"I was going to tell you," I told him.

"Yeah, right. I've heard that one before." Andy switched over to being Mr. Police Officer and he confiscated the bagged lei. His eyes then fixed upon Sophie's phone.

"You're not going to take that," I said. We'd had some past run-ins involving him illegally seizing cell photos.

"Well, then Airdrop that photo to mine."

I attempted to make the photo transfer, but Sophie pulled her phone from my grasp. "I can do it," she said. As a teenager, Sophie had become even more cantankerous and strong-willed. Baachan had commented recently that she was turning out to be exactly like me, but both of us pretended that we didn't hear her.

Chapter Two

Since Mom spent her days hunched over her sewing machine, I was in charge of making dinner every night. Emily occasionally took breaks from her classes, but because of her studies, she really couldn't help. No one was thrilled with my cooking, especially me. My musubi looked like wet melting snowballs, and nobody could figure out how I could burn eggs, but I did.

With everyone still twittering about today's excitement at the beach even after Andy had left, I started to think about meal prep for tonight's dinner. I returned the empty plastic bowls and spoons on a tray back to the shack. After tossing the trash, I pulled out a whole chicken from the refrigerator. That food was for the needy, and it turns out that our family qualifies. I didn't bother to share that we were recipients of the food bank with the rest of the family, especially my father, because they would feel uncomfortable about receiving aid. But we had seven mouths to feed and hardly any income, so I was going to do what I could to keep us alive.

I trudged past my family; they were too engaged with themselves to notice me. I crossed the highway toward the sloping hills toward Waimea Canyon. The perfume of white ginger filled my nostrils. White blooms weighed down the angel trumpet trees. Giant bumpy green ovals of jackfruit hung down from branches, and mangoes were making their final appearance of the season. Without the cars pumping their exhaust on the highway circling Kaua'i, the sunsets were more beautiful than ever. It seemed as though the land, sea, and sky were celebrating the absence of outsiders. And to tell you the truth, many of the local people were happy as well.

A familiar white van stopped by my side.

"Hop in, I'll give you a ride." Sean was wearing a skyblue disposable medical mask, his curly brown hair down to his shoulders. He resembled a young Greek god instead of what he really was—a Jewish geek from Silicon Valley. "You can sit in the back if you don't want to be too close."

I shook my head, pulling up my mask. My chicken in my right hand, I lifted myself into the front of his van with my left.

Sean Cohen and I hadn't started off as friends. In fact, Kelly and I had first suspected that he was a serial killer, driving around in his suspicious white van with California plates. He kept the van, but traded the plates for Hawai'i ones. My whole family—well, all the female members, at least—had developed an attachment to him. I wasn't quite sure, however, where I stood.

In the beginning of the pandemic, Sean and I saw a lot of each other. The businesses in Waimea Junction met to figure out what to do while tourism was shut down. Sean announced that he was going to waive our rents for at least six months. Despite his generosity, Pekelo wasn't impressed. He and Kelly, whose given name was Kūheakapu, were kānaka maoli, native Hawaiians, and he viewed any outsider, especially a haole landlord from California, with suspicion.

"Heard that you may have saved a woman's life," Sean said as he steered up the hill.

"Word gets around fast."

"I was at the hospital, getting a COVID test."

"Sammie," I said, predicting the source of the gossip.

"Andy Mabalot says for me to go get a test today too."

"You should. Just in case. This is my tenth test."

"That's because you are flying all over."

"Probably heading to Oʻahu in the next couple of days."

"Mayor keeping you busy?"

"Anything to help the Islands."

"Must be nice to get away."

Sean must have sensed my underlying anxiety. "How are you doing?"

"Kinda shook me," I told him. I didn't realize how triggering it had been to see that unconscious woman. Just last year I had discovered a body on the floor of the shave ice shack—only, that body did not come back to life.

"I bet. We all have enough going on."

I swallowed and took a deep breath, feeling the coldness of the chicken on my belly through my T-shirt. When I first returned to Kauaʻi, the panic attacks that had plagued me at the university in Seattle had subsided. But around May of this year, they had reemerged, keeping me up at night. Only when Emily returned from Santa Clara had they disappeared. I was happy to give up my bed and sleep on the floor for the comfort of her presence. Now, with the appearance of this drowning woman, a familiar anxiety buzzed in my gut.

Sean respectfully stayed in his van as I jumped onto the driveway of our house. Truth be told, we would have welcomed him inside, but I knew I had to use my head: Mom had multiple sclerosis, and getting COVID would be a complication that she might not survive. Even within the household, we all limited close contact with her, as both

Dani and Sophie were going in to school a couple of days a week.

"I think I'm getting another shipment of food tomorrow," he said.

"What time?"

"Ten thirty in the morning."

"I'll be there."

"You sure? It's just that I have to be in Līhu'e tomorrow."

"No worries."

As his van's back tires spit out red dirt and gravel as he left the street, I remembered the footage from the security cameras. I had forgotten to follow up with him about that, but I figured Andy must have contacted him by now.

I could have walked to the hospital, but I knew the tests were administered in patients' cars. It was a wonder that our Ford Fiesta was still operating; but at least during the pandemic, I wasn't putting many more miles on it. Ever since turning fifteen, Sophie had been bugging me about giving her driving lessons, but I was resisting. To risk my life with her behind the wheel was one more stress I didn't need.

The local hospital was small by Mainland standards. In fact, on the whole island, we only had nine ICU beds. That's why the mayor was trying to keep the COVID cases down to practically zero.

"Howzit, Sammie," I said to a figure standing on the curb near a sign telling all patients to stop for a COVID test. I could barely recognize her, as she was completely covered in a light-blue disposable gown, blue mask, and clear plastic visor. Only her wild hair tamed into a bun gave a clue of her identity. I couldn't quite believe that this woman who was constantly coming in to work late was now in the business of saving lives.

"Andy told me you'd be coming in." She handed me a slip of paper to fill out my name, telephone number, and medical provider. "Fill this in and give it to Ted." I assumed Ted was the masked haole nurse who stood about ten feet away, next to medical supplies in a cart.

"Wait for me after you finish and we can talk story a little."

I nodded. I had some questions for Sammie as well. I filled out the form and proceeded forward.

"Here you go, Ted," I said as I extended my arm out my open window to give him my form.

A frown line appeared above his mask. He took my information and returned with a long cotton swab wand encased in plastic.

"I'm going to first take a sample from the back of your throat," he said. Ted's voice was low and deep, with a country twang.

I opened my mouth wide as he tickled the back of my tongue with the wand. He then placed the same wand up my left nostril. Uji! I was afraid to move, in case he accidentally took a piece of my brain with him. He carefully placed my sample in a vial that held clear liquid. Everything went into the plastic bag. Easy peasy.

"Thanks," I told him, but he was already back at his medical cart.

I drove forward and stopped in front of Sammie, who was waiting for me at the curb. No one was waiting behind me, so we had a free moment.

"How's everyting?" I asked her.

"Kinda worried about the surge. Everyone in the hospital is."

"Is dat really gonna happen on Kaua'i? No cases right now, right?"

"With travel openin' up, who knows?"

"How's the wahine who we fished out of Waimea Bay?"

"Oh, your lady?" Sammie hesitated. "She's still in the ICU. I can't say much. Watch news."

Sammie had chosen a most inconvenient time—at least for me—to be discreet.

Ted was waving his arms toward Sammie, informing her that a new test-taker had arrived.

"I gotta go, Leilani. You'll probably get your results in a couple of days."

As I drove away, I felt good that I had been tested. But what if I had contracted it? I'd probably be referred to as Patient X on websites and Facebook group pages. The last thing the Santiago family needed was another black mark.

Monday

Chapter Three

THE NEXT DAY, I woke up early for me, about nine. There was already a big pot of coffee waiting for me, compliments of probably Baachan. Now that I had broken up with my Seattle boyfriend, Travis, I wasn't receiving any special roasts from the Pacific Northwest, but I hardly missed them. I had gotten to know the coffee companies on Kaua'i and the neighboring islands from the shave ice business. Local coffee had definitely grown on me.

I heard the sound of morning shows coming out of Baachan's back bedroom. In the *before* days, Baachan would have been hanging out in the kitchen, engaging in talk story with me and whoever would listen. But ironically, with us all trapped in the house, we seemed to have siloed away in our respective corners. Mom rarely came out of her bedroom, where her sewing machine was stashed. It was safer for her to be semi-quarantined, anyway. And when they weren't physically in school two times a week, the girls, wearing headphones, sat at their computers on different sides of their shared bedroom. Emily had to make her online classes, which were on California time. She was usually out the door before I was up on Mondays. Since our Wi-Fi connection would get overloaded, she'd head over to the shave ice shack, where she had set up a desk by the window.

I poured coffee into my University of Washington tumbler and slipped on my Crocs by the door. When I'd first moved back to Kaua'i last year, getting up to go to Santiago Shave Ice had been pure drudgery. What person who goes to college on the Mainland—okay, maybe I didn't finish—wants to make shave ice for a bunch of tourists? This wasn't my career path. But I was here to help the family. Then, out of nowhere came the idea: combine shave ice with my passion, coffee. Once those two came together, I was practically running to work in the morning. I repainted the ice shack white with brown trim and borrowed tropical flowers from Court to spruce up the place. Now we were looking like a high-tone haole place à la Joanna Gaines. I even ended up in a local magazine with the headline "Kaua'i Woman Perks Up Shave Ice Business." I was making good.

Sean helped me write a business plan to submit to local banks. I dreamed of opening other shave ice pop-ups on other parts of the island, with the ultimate goal to expand to the Mainland and even Japan. But that was the past, of course. It was *before*.

Now, at twenty-five, I was stringing flowers, something Dani or maybe even a monkey could do. I should have felt more grateful for a source of some money, but frankly I was making more when I was a barista in Seattle during my sophomore year at UW. So I had come full circle: from hating to go to Santiago Shave Ice, to loving it, to now hating it again. As a weekly food distribution center, we were helping our community, which made me feel good at times. But there was one time too many when someone was complaining about what we were offering for free (!) and trying to make swapping deals—*I'll give you two evaporated milks and fruit cocktail for one can of Spam.* I never was that good with customer service, which is probably a deadly failing when your business relies on customers.

My Crocs literally pounded the asphalt as I trudged down our hill. I felt my middle jiggle underneath my T-shirt, which was getting a little too tight. I hated myself for not taking care of myself. But some days I wondered what the point was.

I took a big glug of my coffee before crossing the highway. In the *before* times, it got a bit busy at the end of the day, immediately after the sun set over Waimea Canyon. The canyon, referred to as Hawai'i's Grand Canyon, had a hushed beauty, as if all the secrets would be released at twilight. If you stayed quiet, you could hear the birds twittering and smell the plumeria as an early evening breeze brushed against your cheeks. This was the time, not for fourteen-day tourists, but for we the kama'āina who actually lived on the 'aina, the land, to experience.

Across the way, sweeping the front of the flower shop, was Court's mother, Mrs. Lee, who was wearing her trademark A-line housedress. Mr. and Mrs. Lee were older, in their seventies. They were almost old enough to be my parents' parents, since my mom had me so young. Mr. Lee was born in Hawai'i, and his parents were too. His family were true-blue kama'āina, but their roots went back to South Korea. Mrs. Lee had actually come from South Korea in the 1960s.

They both were tall with long faces, nothing like the petite and delicate Court. Court had been left as a newborn at a local firehouse, and the Lees had adopted her. When we were young, Court loved to speculate who her birth parents might be. "Maybe I'm Native Hawaiian," she'd say hopefully.

"Could be," I said. Some of her features seemed Pacific Islander, but sometimes in a certain light she looked a bit haole. Before she obsessed more, I usually stopped her. "Court, no matta. You Court," I'd declare. "No one like you." Which was the absolute truth.

In spite of the pandemic and the ocean breezes, Mrs. Lee's hair was curled and coiffed perfectly. It was a wonder that the humidity never seemed to affect her appearance.

"Good morning, Auntie," I greeted her as I maintained a respectful distance. Both of us weren't bothering to wear our masks. I had actually forgotten mine at home, but there were plenty of extra ones in the shack.

"Leilani, you looking healthy today."

I knew that was Mrs. Lee's code for saying that I'd gained weight.

"You okay?" I asked her. Kaua'i had prided itself for containing the virus. We only had sixty cases up to this time, and no one had died so far. But now it was opening up, and Waimea had been invaded by a mysterious visitor, the floating woman we Santiago sisters had saved.

"Nothing can hurt me," she said. Come to think of it, I couldn't remember a time when Mrs. Lee had been sick. "Mr. Lee, though, not doing so good."

I looked into the flower shop, and a maskless Mr. Lee was hunched over the desktop computer. His hair was all salt-and-pepper and shaggy, no different than usual. He had fought in the Vietnam War and eschewed any hair style that reminded him of his military years.

I grabbed one of the disposable blue masks that Court kept in front of the store and fastened the loops over my ears.

"Uncle, howzit?"

Mr. Lee stared at me without speaking and returned to the screen, communicating that I needed to take a look. I didn't want to get too close to him, but it was obvious that he wasn't budging from his seat. Turning my face away from him, I tried to focus on the webpage he was showing me. All I could clearly make out was the headline: "Visitor Hospitalized from Lethal Lei."

What the hell? This was irresponsible journalism at its worst. And I was mortified to see that the byline belonged to my sorta friend, Taylor Ogura, originally from New York City.

I took a few steps back from him. "No worries, Uncle. I go handle fo' you."

When I left him, he was murmuring "fake news."

Before I unlocked the door of the shave ice shack, I quickly texted Taylor: *WTF? I thought U were better than that.* I was about to look for the story on my phone when a U-Haul truck drove into our parking lot. I waved to indicate that I was there for the drop-off. After parking, a haole man emerged from the driver's side. "You Leilani?" he asked, and I nodded. He explained that he worked in the hotel industry and was picking up foodstuffs from various hotels that were close to expiring but still good. He opened the back, revealing chips in individual packets, granola bars, and sweetened condensed milk. There were also giant containers of crushed pineapple and tuna—good for large families like ours.

I grew up on the island, but Mainlander Sean had made connections that I never could. He was active in Facebook groups, Twitter, and Instagram. Before the pandemic, he sat in various meetings with the powerful titans of the island, the real estate executives and government officials. So when the people needed more resources than the long-standing food banks could offer, Sean could quickly call other rich people for help.

The driver and I worked quickly and efficiently. He stayed inside the U-Haul and pushed boxes to the edge while I hefted them into the shack. We were finished in probably fifteen minutes. He lowered the door on the truck and gestured for me to wait. From the passenger's side, he gathered a bunch of items encased in plastic and left them on top of our picnic table. "My mother works in hospice, and a couple of her past clients donated these." They were blue hospital gowns, gloves, and even a couple of plastic visors. I hoped there was no need for such drastic protection, but you never know.

"Be safe," he said, flashing the shaka sign.

It was a bit hokey, but I returned the sentiment with my own shaka. Hokeyness felt like a gift during these times.

As soon as the U-Haul left, I was back on my phone. Taylor had responded to my text: *The killer lei story?*

Yup.

I can call or Zoom later today.

To hell with Zoom, I thought. I felt like a fool talking to a laptop.

No, in person, I texted back.

I'm on a story at Lydgate.

K. See you in 40 min.

I grabbed a granola bar and some Cheez-Its from the food pantry. Not the most nutritious midday meal, but it would have to do. I didn't bother to say anything to Emily, who was wearing her expensive noise-canceling headphones for her Zoom class. I took out my father's scooter from the back of Killer Wave. I'd only ridden it once during the pandemic, and there was still gas in its tank. I pulled on a helmet and powered the motor.

Chapter Four

For Taylor to be at Lydgate Beach Park meant only one thing: she was doing a story on the homelessness on the island. There were some official homeless beaches on Kaua'i now—Lydgate Park, Anini on the North Shore, and Salt Pond Beach Park, which was about ten miles from Waimea. Since I was mostly staying close to home, there hadn't been much reason for me lately to drive to Lydgate, which was about thirty miles northeast and close to Wailua. I prayed that the scooter would make it, but then, my father had driven it all the way to Hanalei in the past, so I was hopeful.

Taylor, wearing her trademark black blazer, was leaning against her old tan Toyota, which looked as plain and unadorned as she was. She wore no makeup, and her preference of dress was either this same blazer or an oversized T-shirt. Her skin was white as rice, and I don't think she'd ever worn a bathing suit since coming to Kaua'i from New York City. I wondered about her sexuality sometimes, but it never was a topic of discussion, especially since I myself hadn't had sex for the past year and a half.

I waved to her as I drove down the line of tents and parked SUVs, in which families were now presumably living.

By the time I'd parked the scooter, Taylor was already by the side of the road. It was spooky how swiftly she could travel without being detected.

I refastened my medical mask as I neared her. "I haven't been here in months. Didn't know it was this bad."

Taylor ignored my comment as if it were inconsequential. "What's up?"

Since she wanted to cut to the chase, I went there. "What the hell was that story?"

"Did you read it?"

I hesitated and shook my head.

"That's the problem with you people. Never read."

If anyone else put me in the category of "you people," I would have been offended. But I knew that in Taylor's case, she literally meant "people," as in all human beings.

"I didn't need to read it. *Killer lei*? Clickbait."

"I know. I didn't write the headline. I'm getting it changed. See—they've already done it." Taylor held her phone screen to me. The headline now read "Unidentified Woman Hospitalized after Discovery in Waimea Bay."

I was thankful for the change and looked up the story on my phone.

"Why is the lei even mentioned?"

"There were blisters all over her chest. It's called margarita dermatitis. It's like a second-degree burn."

I remembered the eruptions on the woman's skin. "And that can kill someone?"

"Well, maybe that's why she went into the water. To get some relief."

The theory was thin, too thin to be in a news report.

"And look, the name of the flower shop isn't mentioned."

"Come on." I quickly skimmed the story on my phone. "A flower shop in Waimea. There's only one. Everyone on the island is gonna know which one." I lowered the phone and looked Taylor in the eye. "So, who is she?"

"Who?"

"You know who. If you're going to cause all this trouble for the Lees, at least tell me who this mystery woman is. I saved her life, you know."

"Oh, it was you." Taylor scribbled something in her notebook.

"Don't mention me in your stories."

"But you'd be the good Samaritan."

"I don't want to be the good anything. If you want me as a source, keep me out of it."

Taylor exhaled. Now knowing that I was involved in the story, she probably figured that she had to give me something. "Okay. The police are waiting for the family to be notified. But her name is Yumi Hara."

"Yumi. She Japanese?" She looked more Pacific Islander to me.

"She has a Japanese passport. She'd been cited on the North Shore for breaking quarantine. She was staying at an Airbnb in Hanalei."

"She by herself?"

Taylor nodded. "She's a travel agent with one of the big companies in Japan."

"She's crazy to be here during a pandemic."

"Hawai'i has officially opened up. But the word is that Kawakami is going to enforce the quarantine again."

"Can he do that?"

"He's gone to the governor for permission."

Maybe she came here early to scope updated travel opportunities. The debates about tourism had become contentious on Kaua'i. On the one hand, we kama'āina realized that the land needed a rest from outside visitors. But on the other hand, people like us depended on tourism to feed our families. I felt as divided as the island itself.

"The thing is—why did she come all the way to Waimea to order a mokihana lei? Curious, right?" Taylor said.

"Who knows, the Japanese are into weird shit." Since both Taylor and I were of Japanese ancestry (me from Baachan), we could be perfectly honest with each other.

"Well, more people in Japan are studying hula than in Hawai'i."

"Maybe this Yumi wanted to see the best place for leis on the island."

"Yeah, maybe." Taylor didn't seem to buy my theory.

I surveyed all the tents and people living out of their cars. Families were cooking on camping stoves and eating white bread sandwiches. My heart felt heavy. Through most of the pandemic, I'd stayed in Waimea. Sure, I saw the people lining up at our food bank, but I never imagined that so many people had lost their homes and were struggling financially.

"What's going to happen to Kaua'i after all this?" It was like I was talking to myself, because Taylor was reading texts on her phone. Her mind was off onto the next story.

"See you, Taylor," I said in a loud voice, jolting her from her phone scrolling.

"Okay, Leilani. Remember to call me if you hear anything new about why Yumi was in Waimea."

"Sure," I lied. It wasn't like I wasn't going to share anything with her. But I was like a competitor on the reality show *Survivor*—I wasn't going to give up anything unless I could benefit from the trade. My years on the Mainland and working at a high-tech company in Seattle had trained me well.

Since I was this far away on the island anyway, I continued to drive north on my scooter. It still was unreal how the highway was so deserted. As I rode along the coastline, I felt that the 'aina was talking to me. *Keep me safe. Give me more time to heal.*

The air slapped against my bare thighs and my helmet. I had been overwhelmed by what I saw at Lydgate Beach Park. I couldn't process what our future might be, because the present day was so alien.

I passed the gutted Coco Palms Resort, now only concrete squares from the destruction back in 1992 from Hurricane Iniki. There were still plenty of cars parked at Safeway Market, making it seem that not much had changed. A few minutes later, I reached downtown Kapa'a, our version of an Old Town tourist destination. During the height of the tourist season, people carrying their drinks and shave ice would be jaywalking through the main intersection. Now, so many restaurants were closed. I checked to see that Déjà Vu Surf, which goes back more than a hundred years to a Japanese immigrant confectionery shop, was still open. Technically, Déjà Vu was Killer Wave's competitor, but during this time we were all one 'ohana.

By this time, my stomach was starting to rumble, bigtime. I made a quick stop along the highway for a deepfried malasada. That's when I first noticed the motorcycle, which was stopped about a hundred yards away. The rider was dressed in black, including a black leather jacket, which didn't make sense in Hawai'i. He was wearing a tinted helmet, too, so I couldn't see his face.

I didn't have a credit card with me—only a crumpled five-dollar bill in my pocket, enough to pay for one malasada. I felt a pang of guilt over not being able to treat the whole family back at the house. But once I bit into that soft, fluffy doughnut outside and tasted the gooey custard in the middle, my guilt miraculously disappeared.

I was holding on to the other half of the malasada when I got back on the scooter. I turned the key to the ignition, and as I putt-putted onto the highway, the same motorcycle came at me with tremendous speed. It pushed me off the road into some long weeds, causing the half malasada to fall custard first onto the dirt. "Damn you!" I shouted.

The motorcycle continued down the highway as if I didn't exist. It left behind an awful-smelling plume of black smoke. I don't know which made me more upset—that this jerk ran me off the highway, or that I had lost my sugary treat. I would have assumed that he was a careless tourist, but tourists usually didn't drive beat-up motorcycles that backfire.

I was in a bad mood as I neared Waimea Junction. Between the homeless encampment and the rude encounter with the unknown motorcyclist, I was beginning to wonder if the Kaua'i that I knew had changed forever. The door of Lee's Leis and Flowers was open, and I hoped Court was around so I could at least talk story with her and sort out my thoughts. During business hours, the Lees kept both the front and back doors ajar so breezes could travel through the store, a natural antidote to any airborne viruses that might be hanging around. I parked the scooter in the back of Killer Wave, leaving the helmet on its seat, and poked my head into the flower shop.

Sure enough, Court was by herself, sitting at the main table.

I reached for one of the disposable masks that they kept by the door for customers, but Court shook her head.

"Don't bother, Leilani. We family."

I knew that "being family" wasn't enough to ward off COVID, but for a moment I wanted to escape to the *before* times, when two lifelong BFFs could freely talk story.

I sat at the other end of the table, feeling the breeze blow through my overgrown hair.

Court was one of these women whose hands were always busy. If she wasn't stringing leis, she was typing on her keyboard or doing hand-stitch work. But now she was sitting still, her palms flat on the table, as if she had surrendered.

"What's wrong?"

"I want to show you something." She opened her laptop and passed it to me. On her screen was a frozen image of what looked like the front of the flower shop. "Before, I thought dat woman just did self-serve on Sunday—picked up her lei from our table outside." Everything was by the honor system with customers at Waimea Junction. We figured that if you had to steal something, you probably needed it more than we did. "Well, Sean emailed the security footage from Sunday morning. Dat's da lady, Yumi Hara. She's talking to somebody. It wasn't self-serve."

I pressed the arrow for play, and the camera showed the top of her head and side of her face, enough for her clear identification. But the video didn't show the person in the shop who she was talking to. "No audio?"

Court shook her head.

"Who could it have been?" I asked, more to myself than Court.

"You were at the flower shop dat morning."

"Yeah, around ten." Court's parents and Kelly were all there by the time I arrived.

"Does the video have time code?"

"Yup. It was nine a.m."

I wasn't sure when each person had arrived before me.
"Did you ask Kelly?"

"He says dat he nevah see her."

"And your parents?"

"They said no."

"But Yumi obviously saw someone." That security footage proved that someone at Lee's did, in fact, see her. If it wasn't those three, who had it been?

I remained quiet. I heard the hum of their floral refrigerator and maybe a rooster in the distance.

"And now dat baka online story. Written by your friend."

"She's not really my friend."

That didn't win Court over.

"I talked wit her already," I said. "I met her at Lydgate."

"Lydgate? What's dere?"

"She doin' a story of homelessness during the pandemic."

"Oh, yah." A line of concern marked Court's otherwise smooth forehead. "Bad ova dere?"

"Looks like lots of people in trouble. And I was almost driven off the road by some lolo motorcyclist."

"What?" That really got a rise out of Court.

"You know anyone with an old motorcycle that backfires?"

"That could be anyone in Waimea. Half of the guys in our high school class."

"Yeah." I told myself to let go of that random encounter. "Anyway, I set the reporter straight. The headline was bad. She made them change it, by the way."

That didn't mitigate Court's anger.

To be honest, it wasn't like the flower shop phone was ringing off the hook, anyway, during the pandemic. I knew

Court enough that her strong feelings were not about business. "What's wrong?" I repeated, but in a louder voice.

"I'm scared. We had a tele-meeting with the obstetrician."

I waited. *Please, don't let anytin be wrong with da baby.*

"I mean, I'm on schedule But Mom can't be with me when I deliver."

"How about Kelly?"

"Yah, he can be in dere. Only one person." Under normal circumstances, we all would have been crowded in her hospital room after her delivery. My dad would have brought in an ice cooler filled with beer and soda, while Mom and I would have made trayfuls of Spam musubi.

We would have had a party right then and there. It did feel sad and lonely to be in a virtually empty room to welcome a new life.

"Well, at least you have Kelly."

Court gripped the surface of the table. "He's changed."

"Well, he gonna be a fadda."

"Yeah, but I dunno. He hasn't been sleeping. I'll wake up to go shi-shi—and I have to go a lot now—and he'll be up, staring at the computer."

"Video games?"

Court didn't bother responding to my sarcastic comment. "He stopped going to church. I mean, the virtual kine. I tell him he doesn't even have to wear pants to watch with me. But he say no. He even leaves the room when he hears that I have it on."

Kelly had been a devoted Christian ever since high school, and I was surprised that he was rejecting his faith at a time like this.

"And what's going on with Emily?" she asked.

"Whatchu mean?'

"I heard that she's been spending a lot of time with Pekelo. Going over to Hanalei like regular."

I twisted a piece of my hair around my finger. My hair had become as dry as the ends of an old banana leaf. I didn't like the idea of Emily spending so much time with Kelly's brother, either. I had nothing against Pekelo, but he was adrift in his life. Maybe he reminded me of myself, so I wanted to keep my distance from him. Even more so for Emily, who was moving on to bright, better things in California.

I stood up and stretched my legs, which were starting to cramp up from my long scooter ride. I walked over to the refrigerator case and gazed at the row of cut flowers in vases. A couple of birds of paradise, bunches of red carnations, a lot of greens. In a box, a few green mokihana berries.

"Did you know about the mokihana being poison?"

"Of course. I'm sensitive about it myself. Kelly da one who makes dem. But we always tell the customer not to wear on bare skin. I told dat lady when she came to order on Saturday, but she didn't seem to speak English. When she picked up on Sunday, she shoulda been told again." Court picked up a square Styrofoam oasis left on the work table. It was dark green like the leaves of a plant.

"Dis whole killer lei thing will blow ova," I told Court. "Thanksgiving time, Christmas, people be ordering their floral arrangements again."

"Yah, you probably right, Leilani. You always right." Court smiled faintly, but I wasn't fooled. We both knew deep inside that I didn't know what I was saying.

The sun was starting to go down as I walked up the hill to our house. I felt weary, full of doubts and with more questions than answers. As I neared the house, our rooster Jimin's crowing got louder. More than annoying, it sounded plaintive, as if Jimin was signaling that a disaster was rounding the corner.

As soon as I entered the house and removed my Crocs, Emily rose from the living room table. She closed her laptop and seemed ready to go somewhere.

"Everyone's fed," she said.

"Thanks."

"We made somen salad. Used up all the kamaboko. We saved some for you in the fridge."

"Thanks." Sometimes the family had to fill in and make dinner, which was a relief to me and probably them.

I made a beeline for the refrigerator and pulled out a glass bowl. On a bed of white skinny noodles were strips of shiitake mushrooms and omelet, topped with chopped green onion, red ginger, and a generous sprinkle of furikake. It was flavored with a shoyu sauce, salty and garlicky. As I closed the fridge, I noticed there wasn't much else left on the shelves now. Just a large carton of eggs. Thank God for eggs.

After selecting a pair of red chopsticks from our hashi mug, I took my somen salad into the living room and sat cross-legged in front of the living room table.

I must have been shoveling too many noodles into my mouth, because Emily made note of it. "You're eating like you're starving."

"I haven't eaten all day." Except for the food bank junk food and half of the malasada.

"So what were you doing?"

"Food delivery at the shack. Then I had words with Taylor Ogura."

"Who?"

I keep forgetting that Emily had become unfamiliar with my life on Kauaʻi while she'd been at school. "Oh, she's the reporter who wrote the 'killer lei' story. She got the headline changed, at least."

Emily shook her head. "I didn't see it."

Our conversation felt stilted, like we were both throwing rocks at the ocean but never connecting. At one time we'd been inseparable, our legs tangled as we sat at the beach or on one of our beds. Emily had become a bit of a stranger now—more polished, ambitious, self-directed.

"I'm going to take the car, okay?"

My right cheek was filled with a ball of the somen noodles. "What for?" I asked.

Emily paused. We both knew where she was going.

"Em, what are you doing with him?" *You too good for Pekelo,* I want to say to her. But once she started law school, our dynamics had changed. No longer was I the leader of the Santiago sisters. She had taken that place—not because she had forced me off the throne, but because I had ceded it.

"Don't worry about me. I can take care of myself." Emily slipped her laptop into her backpack and went to retrieve the Ford car keys that I'd hung on a hook by the front door.

I knew there was nothing I could say to change her mind. Kahuakai men were like chewed gum: when they stuck on the soles of your rubbah slippahs, they were hard to remove.

Tuesday

Chapter Five

THE NEXT MORNING, Emily was fast asleep in the bed, gurgling in short bursts like water rushing into tidepools. I felt for my phone and checked the time. Seven a.m. I pulled the sleeping bag off myself and rubbed my eyes. I don't know why I was up. There was no reason to be awake so early. It was another day of the pandemic, one day merging into another, Groundhog Day with no end. Except Yumi Hara had entered my life. And for some reason she had become the pebble in my Croc, reminding me that everything was not quite the same.

I couldn't fall back to sleep, and I staggered out of my windowless dungeon. As soon as I opened my bedroom door, a flood of light blinded me. I smelled coffee—it was probably a new batch I'd ordered from the Big Island. On our Formica kitchen tabletop was a Tupperware container holding fresh lavender-colored poi, a gift from Pekelo, no doubt.

This poi was not the weak, white, soupy kind served to tourists at hotel luaus. It had substance and heft. Personality. This was the expensive stuff.

Probably sensing that I was about to open up the Tupperware, Baachan appeared. Her hair looked more frightening than mine, resembling a long cone of an 'amakihi nest.

She looked me over from crazy mop top to uji toenails. "You getting fat like one sumo wrestler."

"You for talk." Even her mu'umu'u couldn't hide her waistline, which was expanding like rising bread dough.

After our exchange of insults, both of us felt better. I gestured to the open Tupperware tub. "You want for breakfast?"

Baachan poked her finger in the poi and tasted. "Not sour."

"Dis the fresh stuff." I spooned two generous portions in two bowls and searched the cabinets for a good accompaniment. Jackpot! Canned sardines, barely expired. Baachan's favorite.

We ate without speaking, sitting on different sides of the table. I was waiting for my COVID test result, but I felt fine, symptom-free. Jimin squawked in the backyard. I closed my eyes and savored this moment. I traveled back to a time when mornings meant the start of unexpected possibilities and not the same familiar rerun.

I was halfway through my poi when Sophie stumbled into the kitchen, dark bags under her eyes. I thought maybe the smell of the sardines had led her to the kitchen. She was wearing the same T-shirt and shorts that she'd worn the day before.

"You playing video games all night again?"

She didn't answer my question. "Is Emily up?"

"She had a late night."

Sophie remained standing in front of me. I was obviously her second choice for help.

I glared back at her, hoping she'd slink back into her bedroom.

"What is it?" I finally asked.

"Ro."

"What about her?" Ro had been Sophie's best friend since kindergarten. While Sophie had too many faults to count, she was a loyal friend. I acknowledged that much.

"She hasn't been in class for a few days now. She always was at our classes at school on Monday. On our Google days, she used to log in without her video, and now notting."

"She sick?"

"I dunno. She doesn't have a cell phone, and no one picks up the phone at her house."

"Maybe your teacher can look into it?"

Sophie was biting some skin on the edge of her thumb, which was turning as red as a cherry tomato from the abuse. I knew something was seriously wrong.

"You want me to check on her?"

"You can?"

I glanced at my phone. "School's gonna start in fifteen. You check in on the computer and I'll take care of Ro."

Sophie remained at my side.

"What?"

"I kinda let her borrow someting."

"Like what?"

"Our tent."

"What for?"

"She said just for fun."

From my adult point of view, a tent did not mean fun: it meant escape. From where and why was Ro seeking escape?

I got into the Ford without taking a shower first. The one advantage of social distancing and masks was that people didn't see the status of your teeth or get bothered by your body odor. At least I hoped Mrs. Ramos, Ro's mother, didn't have a keen sense of smell.

Ro didn't like us to come to her house, so I'd usually pick her up from the school and take her to ours. She and her parents used to live closer to us, but since Ro's father had disappeared, Mrs. Ramos moved to her maternal grandmother's house in Hanapepe, about seven miles from us.

The house was more ramshackle than I remembered. It was super-small, only a couple of bedrooms and probably under a thousand square feet. Our little house was no palace either, but at least we were surrounded by mango trees. Ro's house was hemmed in by dead brown grass and a chainlink fence. Even the Kaua'i correctional facility had more signs of life.

I opened the waist-high gate and proceeded to the front door, which was protected by a security gate. Hardly any homes in our neighborhood had bars on their windows or doors.

I pushed the doorbell, but the buzzer seemed disconnected from any electrical source. I instead dragged my keys against the metal gate. "Hello, is anyone home?" I said through my mask.

The door finally opened to reveal a bleary-eyed Mrs. Ramos, who was—no surprise—maskless. There were dark rings around her eyes, and her skin was a sallow yellow color. She did not look good.

"Who you? You from DCFS?"

I didn't know what concerned me most: That Ro's mother didn't recognize me, or that she would immediately assume that I was from the Department of Children and Family Services. I tried to give her the benefit of the doubt and blamed her lack of recognition on my mask and the early hour.

"Mrs. Ramos, it's me, Leilani. Leilani Santiago, Sophie's older sister."

"Oh, you."

Mrs. Ramos had known me since Ro was five years old.

"Sophie's been worried that Ro hasn't been in school."

"And what can I do about that? We have no Wi-Fi. How can my girl even do her studies without all this fancy computer stuff?"

"I think the school may have some hotspots."

Mrs. Ramos frowned, confused by the technical lingo. "She sits in da McDonald's parking lot on Google class days. Maybe she dere right now."

I tried to look past Mrs. Ramos's shoulder into her house. "Did she sleep here last night?"

A barrel-chested man in a Jack Daniels T-shirt came from behind Mrs. Ramos. "Marian, what's going on?"

"Oh, dis Roger."

Roger had a thick mane of black hair that looked like it had been oiled down maybe a few days earlier. He was incredibly hairy, with several days' growth of a full beard that went down to the middle of his neck. I didn't know what kind of work Roger did, if he did at all, but personal cleanliness was obviously not required.

"The girl's wild. There's no tellin' where she might be." He spoke as if he had marbles in his mouth.

"So you don't know where Ro is?"

"Who you?"

Mrs. Ramos hung on to his shoulder as if she was afraid that I might want to claim him. Really? "Oh, you know Sophie, Ro's friend? Dis is her older sistah."

"The Santiagos, right? Of Santiago Shave Ice? I know your fadda. Went to your house once to pick up some old tools he was giving away."

I shuddered to think that this Roger knew where we lived. He'd probably met my dad before he went sober.

"I think your fadda owes me some money, in fact. We made a bet on a UH game a while back."

"You're gonna have to take it up with him. He's in O'ahu right now." Shit, why did I say that? The less this man knew about us, the better. "Anyway, I was worried about Ro, so I was checking in."

"No worry about her. She's fine."

I mumbled something as I turned away from the door, which slammed shut.

I knew I should immediately report Mrs. Ramos to DCFS. But Sophie would never forgive me. And I wasn't sure that Ro would end up in a better place. If I didn't find her today, however, I would have no choice but to go to the authorities.

In the driver's seat of the Ford, I thought hard. If Ro had asked for a tent, she probably had plans to pitch it somewhere. I imagined her bony frame. She wouldn't have the stamina to go far. Maybe Salt Pond, about a half hour by foot.

I hadn't gone over to Salt Pond since the beginning of the year. Salt Pond was good for families with babies or kids below five. The water was shallow and calm, the perfect paddling pool.

I parked in the open lot and surveyed the landscape. Dried palm-tree fronds lay on the beach. The waterline was still and calm until it seemed to melt into the horizon.

On the side of the shore were rows of tents. In comparison, Lydgate seemed more upscale because half of those folks at least had cars to live in. The Salt Pond settlers seemed to have less—in terms of material possessions and family members.

As I approached the tents, I recognized some of the faces of the people sitting in the sand or carrying water jugs.

"Hey, you da Santiago shave ice girl," one older man called out. His skin was as dark as a koa tree from constant exposure to sun.

"I could use a rainbow ice right now," called out another man, this one younger, with a five o'clock shadow.

Regular customers. I felt sick to my stomach. I saw some of them during our food giveaways, but to see them sleeping in tents along the beach was too much.

I waved and smiled, feeling the sides of my mask lifting up. Mom said some people can smile with their eyes, but I doubted I was one of them. Smiles did not come easily to me. I hated to be fake.

I didn't want to be like a cop and directly ask about Ro. I knew what I was looking for, and on the edge of the homeless encampment I saw it: a familiar small blue tent, shaped like the top of a mushroom. I removed my Crocs as I plowed through the sand to reach my target.

I bent over and looked through the front, which faced the ocean. The outside flap was open, but the inside mesh was zipped shut. She was lying face down, drawing in a notebook. Both she and Sophie had had an unhealthy manga addiction since they were in grade school.

On one side of the tent was a stack of books and her Chrome laptop. Ro had folded a few T-shirts and a hoodie on the other side. There was no sleeping bag or blanket; she was lucky to be so young and be able to deal with a lack of comfort. It reminded me of when Emily and I could make huge sandcastles—pretend homes—around Waimea Bay when we were about Dani's age. We'd dream about living in expansive homes with multiple bedrooms. In her blue bubble, Ro had created a semblance of a home for herself.

She felt the presence of a nearby person and abruptly turned around. "Oh, you wen scare me, Auntie Leilani." She laced her fingers together around her thin chest. Remnants of pink polish were barely visible on her fingernails.

I knelt down in the sand. "Did you sleep here last night?"

Afraid of how to respond, Ro widened her eyes.

"You can't stay here."

"Why? This is a good tent."

"I know." There had been times in which I, weary of all the noise in the house, had pitched this same tent in our backyard to get some peace and quiet.

I unzipped the front mesh and squatted in the tent. The blue fabric made the tent seem like it had merged into both the sky and the sea.

"I no like go home," Ro said.

"Is it because of your mom's boyfriend?"

"No," she said a little too quickly, as if she had anticipated my question.

"I'm not leaving you here. And dis tent ours, anyways."

"I can buy it from you. I can pay in installments."

Her attempt to be independent touched me, especially since there was no way she could come up with the money to pay for it.

"You can stay wid us until we sort dis out."

"Too many Santiagos in your house." That was for sure.

"Well, my father is on O'ahu, so for the time being you can stay with us. We can set up the tent in the backyard, but you have to sleep in Dani and Sophie's room. And when you're not sitting in school, you can take your online classes at Waimea Junction. The Wi-Fi is much stronger there. I'll have to get your madda's permission, though."

"No, can you try wait before tellin' my madda? Just a day or so."

In some ways, I didn't see the harm. Mrs. Ramos didn't seem worried about her only daughter.

Ro gathered her things and stuffed them into a weathered backpack. Once she was out, I collapsed the tent and folded the fabric and fiberglass poles into a narrow duffel bag.

As we walked through the encampment toward my car, an older woman, obviously braless in her tank top, approached us. "You takin' her home? Good for you."

The other members of the makeshift tent city came to our assistance. "It's okay; the tent is super light," I told them; but upon seeing the disappointed looks on their faces, I relented.

The dark-skinned man, his sinewy muscles bulging like tangled tree trunks, took hold of the tent, while the younger one carried Ro's heavy backpack to my car.

Ro said nothing during our drive back to the house. I wasn't sure whether she was annoyed or relieved that she would be staying with us. I sensed it was a combination of both.

Sophie was sitting on the porch with Jimin the rooster strutting in the front yard.

"Ro!" Sophie ran to us and wrapped her left arm around Ro's head. The No. 3 Santiago sister drove me crazy at times, but I did appreciate that, at her heart, she was a protector.

"Help get her stuff from the car," I commanded, and for once Sophie didn't argue. I followed the two girls back to the trunk to retrieve the tent. Ro looked longingly at her overnight home.

"I'll put it up in the backyard for you," I told her. "But don't leave your computer in there. And stay outta Auntie Wendy's room, okay?"

Ro nodded as Sophie pulled her into the house with Ro's backpack. I could see why Ro was a bit resistant to being enfolded into our large clan. For some people, too much love can be damn oppressive.

I carried the tent through the living room, our kitchen, and then our backyard door.

I unfolded the nylon fabric, brushing away the sand from Salt Pond that had accumulated in the tent's corners. After I put it up, I climbed inside it, feeling comforted by the blue enclosure. I covered my eyes with my balled hands. I wanted to cry so bad, but nothing would come out. I felt like a worn rag that had been wrung one too many times. I felt the weight not only of my own losses but my island's too. My phone dinged that I'd received an email and it was a bit of good news. I had tested negative for the virus.

I went inside and grabbed one of my freshly washed masks hanging from a line in the bathroom. I went to the farthest bedroom and knocked on the door before opening.

Mom was at her sewing machine, the light on the machine picking up the vibrant colors of the fabric she was stitching together.

As I entered, she sat back in her chair and took her foot off the machine pedal. I saw the flash of her smile before she adjusted a mask over her mouth and nose. "Leilani, I feel like we never see each other. And here we are, under the same roof."

Since Dad was away for several days, she had transformed the space into a full-fledged sewing room. On her bedspread were rows of freshly sewn masks and a stack of new fabric.

"These are beautiful, Mom."

Baachan's friend from her ukulele class had dropped off some Okinawan cloth. The background was bright yellow, the shade of mustard on a hot dog at a baseball stadium, decorated with red lion dogs and green maple leaves.

"At least I feel like I'm being useful," she said.

"I wish I could say the same."

Lines appeared on Mom's forehead. "Leilani, you're the one who's keeping this family afloat."

"No, Emily—"

"Leilani, it's you. I see you working behind the scenes when nobody's looking. Even though I can't be with you like before, I see you."

Even though I was a grown woman, I wanted my mother's arms around me, consoling me. But it was too dangerous to ask for it now.

I explained that Ro would be staying with us for a few days, and, as I expected, Mom had no problems with an extra body in our already-crowded home. While Mom was a haole girl from Orange County, her heart had become completely kama'āina. What we had could be shared.

I got up, realizing that we were running low on milk and cereal. "I gotta take a quick trip to Big Save Market," I said at the door.

"Be safe, my girl," Mom said.

"You, too."

While making my quick purchases at the market, I thought about Yumi Hara. I didn't even know the woman: why was she on my mind? Was it because I breathed life into her, one of the most sacred expressions of love and respect in Hawai'i?

Or was it because I had nothing better to do these days?

Maybe it was her aloneness, even floating by herself in our Waimea Bay. Even though I was surrounded by people, I felt lonely too. Maybe if I discovered why she was in Kaua'i by herself, I could feel more at peace.

On my way home, I took a detour past the hospital. There was a short line for testing, and while I recognized Sammie's coworker Ted, I didn't see Sammie.

After I was parked back in our driveway, I started texting on my phone.

How's Yumi

No response from Sammie. Damn her.

I lugged two one-gallon plastic jugs of milk and a giant box of generic Cheerios into the kitchen. I was in the middle of moving the food in the refrigerator to make space for the milk when my phone rang.

I closed the refrigerator door. "Hey, Sammie."

"Don't text me about her. I can get in big trouble." Sammie's voice was uncharacteristically sharp. Since I was usually the one upset with her, it felt strange for the tables to be turned.

"C'mon. I've helped you outta more problems than I can count."

Silence. Sammie knew what I was saying was true.

"No change," she finally said.

"What?"

"There's no change with Yumi Hara. She's in a medically induced coma. We're hoping she comes out of it."

I held my phone against my shoulder with the crook of my head as I opened the cereal box. "Any contact from her family?"

"No." Sammie sounded sad that Yumi was so alone in Kaua'i. "But there's a woman dat keeps calling about her status."

"A relative?" Or maybe Taylor.

"I don't think so. She sounds haole. And older."

Taylor was pretty haole-fied, but she pronounced her consonants with a slight softness that revealed her Japanese American background.

"Get her name and contact info for me."

"You ask for too much!"

"Please. Tell her the family who pulled Yumi out of the water wants to know."

"Okay," Sammie finally relented. "If I pick up the phone when she calls, I'll ask her. But dat's all I can promise."

Wednesday

Chapter Six

THE NEXT MORNING, I fumbled for my phone on the floor, which I had left plugged into an outlet overnight.

It was nine, so not too early to be calling our illustrious former Big Apple scribe. I stumbled out of my cave of a bedroom and found Taylor Ogura's phone number.

She answered on the first ring. "What do you want, Leilani?"

Well, aloha to you too, Taylor.

"Do you know what Airbnb Yumi was staying in?"

"The police have already been over there. Talked to the owner and went inside."

"Where is it, Taylor?"

"I don't know about the address. But I know the name of the Airbnb host."

"Well?"

"And what will I get?"

I silently cursed Taylor. Why can't she help without thinking about what she'd get in return? I had to give her something, so I told her this: "There's no change in Yumi's condition. And she doesn't have family, as far as the hospital can tell. But a woman keeps calling the nurses to ask about her. That's not you, is it?"

"I've been going through my contacts in the hospital administration."

Taylor sometimes didn't know how to play it in Hawai'i. Instead of top down, it's often more productive to go bottom up. But I wasn't going to tell her how to do her job.

"Once I get her name and contact information, I'll pass it along to you."

I could feel Taylor's smile through the phone line. After she provided me the Airbnb owner's name, I clicked off without even saying good-bye.

I had an Airbnb account for the times I'd booked places for business contacts from O'ahu to Kaua'i. The offerings for Kaua'i were sparse, compared to the *before* times. Still, there were some listings, especially on the North Shore.

I looked up the hosts for the different rental units. It wasn't difficult to locate the Super Host. In her photo, she had shoulder-length strawberry-blond waves and wore a bright red Hawaiian-print sundress. I had a feeling that she probably lived in California.

When I looked at the calendar for her rental, all of October had been blocked off. Had Yumi Hara booked the entire month? If she had, she had money, that was for sure. The rental fee was $200 a day, so thirty days would cost her $6,000.

I clicked on the various photos of the property. It was expansive, way too large for one person. This Yumi Hara liked to travel in style. Even though I was from Kaua'i, I sometimes became envious of moneyed tourists who experienced my island in five-star comfort.

The property was a full-on single-family detached house, not a condo crammed next to another condo. It looked like it had been built in the 1950s, airy with skylights and multiple windows. In the back was a low louvered window, with horizontal glass panels arranged like Venetian blinds. Court's parents' house had one of those windows, and both of us had become experts in dismantling the panels when we snuck out late on Friday or Saturday nights in high school. Mr. and Mrs. Lee finally figured out what was going on and replaced them with a regular window. Why would a fancy place have a window so vulnerable to break-ins? Waitaminnit, I was thinking like a former Seattleite. This was Kaua'i.

I sent the link to my Uncle Rick, who wasn't a blood relative but my father's best friend. He lived in Hanalei—in fact, Pekelo was renting his guest room right now. Our island was so small that I figured he'd probably be familiar with this property.

Do you know where this house is? I included some screenshots of the exterior.

It only took him two minutes to text me back immediately with a street and the closest intersection.

I texted back: *Mahalo*

Rick: *You coming to Hanalei? Stop by.*

Hanalei was my favorite part of the North Shore. Princeville was too bougie, with weekend golfers and tourists who detested getting their feet dirty when walking to the beach. Hanalei, on the other hand, was more inaka, as Baachan would say. Country and isolated. It was for people who wanted a break from other people. For both good and bad reasons.

Uncle Rick and Auntie Barbara lived there because they were inaka. They liked having a chicken coop in the backyard and fresh eggs in the morning. They liked sitting on their porch with their dog at their side in the mornings, while in the evenings, their 'ōpū full of a home-cooked meal of kalua pig or grilled mahi-mahi, they watched the orange burst of the sunset. It was wetter in Hanalei than Waimea, which meant the green foliage was plentiful, with ferns' coiled fronds beckoning passersby like witches' fingers.

Uncle Rick was now living in the house by himself. I didn't like to think about why that was, and we never talked about it. Auntie Barbara was being "rehabilitated," as the haoles liked to say. Rick was retired from the county, so he used to visit Auntie Barbara in Līhu'e every Wednesday. Now, because of COVID, their visits were exclusively via video, which I'd heard was taking a toll on him.

I followed the GPS to the north side of Hanalei onto a street with small but expensive homes. There were no cars parked in driveways or on the street. I figured most of these were either vacation homes or Airbnbs. It made me a little sick to think that while the shelters near the beach were crowded with people, these pristine homes were absolutely empty.

The GPS took me to the end of the street, a cul-de-sac. Sure enough, it was the same exterior in the photo on the Airbnb page. The property sloped down into a gorgeous garden. A wall of yellow hibiscus lined one side, and I smelled plumeria growing somewhere in the vines of greenery. At the base of the garden was a rectangular fountain, water flowing out from the concrete base and trickling down into an encased pool. This was Eden. I could see why Yumi wanted to stay here.

I crept behind the house to look through the louvered back windows that I'd seen in the online photo. The living room, the walls painted light blue, had cathedral ceilings. The side wall was hung with a large nondescript painting, abstract with inoffensive pastel colors. This Super Host understood exactly what she was selling.

I returned to the car and took out a pair of disposable gloves and disinfectant wipes from the trunk. In addition to toilet paper, paper towels, and water, there had been a run on these items at places like Costco. I'd lined up and fought through the crowds with my shopping cart with all the other lolos. It was like hurricane season. We all lost our minds.

As it turned out, I rarely used the gloves or the wipes. It's not like I was going anywhere besides home and Waimea Junction anyway. But here they came in handy—not for sanitizing, but for concealing my identity.

I removed the window panels one by one with my gloved hands until I'd created a space that was big enough for my body to go through. I left my Crocs outside. No need to dirty up the house. The floors were bamboo and felt cool and smooth against my bare feet. The small kitchen was open, with a breakfast counter that overlooked the living room. Might as well maximize the garden view.

I crept down the hallway. The bathroom had both a shower and a deep Japanese-style tub, an *ofuro*. Baachan would have killed for this. She often spoke of the *ofuro* she'd used as a kid on the plantation—although the *ofuro* she spoke of was lined with aluminum, not the smooth peach ceramic tile like this one had. The shower caddy was filled with luxurious bath and beauty products. The traditional Japanese first showered and cleansed themselves before soaking in the *ofuro*.

There was only one bedroom, but it was large, probably the size of half of our house. A king-size bed. A koa wood desk stood against the wall. There was no laptop, purse, or phone. I figure that the police had taken those items.

The closet, however, still held at least ten pieces of clothing on hangers. Yumi was a size S, and that was in Japanese sizes. That sounded about right. She was small-framed. I still remembered pumping her tiny chest with air. She was so delicate and fragile; afterward, I was afraid I might have broken her in half.

Also in the closet was a rollaway suitcase. There was a tag of a Japanese tour company—maybe the place where Yumi worked? In English was her name, an address in Tokyo, and a cell phone number. I took a quick photo of the information with my phone. I laid the suitcase on its side and opened it up. There was a plastic compartment for underwear; I didn't feel a need to paw through her intimates. Folded into threes were a couple pairs of pants. And then another zippered pouch of printouts from Google Japan searches. I arranged the printouts on the bamboo floor and quickly snapped photos of each with my phone. After I finished, I returned everything back to its original location, zipped closed the suitcase, and sanitized the parts that I'd touched.

After exiting the house through the open window, I replaced the glass panels as carefully as I could. I had a strange feeling that I was being watched and practically jogged out to the street.

I was removing my gloves and stuffing them in the front pocket of my shorts when I heard a loud buzzing above me. Largest bug ever, I thought, dipping down my head to avoid a possible sting. The noisemaker descended until it was at eye level. A damn drone.

A young brown man ran up to me with a controller. "Oh, sorry, sorry." He plucked the drone out of the sky in front of me.

"Were you. . . ?" I asked. My face was flushed, revealing my guilt at breaking and entering.

It turned out that the drone operator was even more flustered than I was. "Sorry, I'm so sorry. I wasn't shooting anything down at this level. Really."

I recalled that some residents had been up in arms about drones, accusing their owners of invading private space and creating a public nuisance. Drones weren't allowed in any of our state parks. I planned to use his possible legal infractions against him until I recognized his sturdy frame, man bun, and warm brown eyes. He was a photographer whom I'd run into at special events. As I approached him, he pulled on the off-white N-95 mask that cupped his prominent nose.

"Hey, aren't you Adam? You work with my friend Court on weddings sometimes. She's with Lee's Flowers in Waimea."

Adam's body relaxed. "Leilani, right? What are you doing over here? Delivering some flowers?"

Thank you, Adam, for giving me the perfect alibi.

"Ah, yeah. No one seems to be at home."

"Mostly rentals around here. That's why this is one of my spots to launch my drone. A bunch of us are shooting stock footage for some extra money." Those were the aerial video shots of Hawai'i that ad agencies liked to use.

"Been bad?"

Adam nodded.

"All these canceled weddings. My business is in the toilet. I've been waiting for some PPP money, but they say don't hold your breath." Adam's drone looked like a giant insect in his hands. "How about you? Don't you have a shave ice shop?"

I swallowed. I'd been in my private bubble and hadn't been forced to express the current status of Santiago's. "I haven't reopened. I figure what's the point?"

We both stood in silence, mourning the closures of our respective businesses.

"It'll pick up," Adam declared. "Vaccines are around the corner."

"So they say." I didn't mean to be so dark, but it was my natural personality.

"Well, *gambatte*, okay?" I figured Adam was from Arizona or someplace like that, but he'd been in Kaua'i long enough to pick up some Japanese, probably from his Japanese clients.

"What else can we do?"

"Hey," he called out before I walked back to the Ford. "Can I get your number? Just in case I get any business leads."

"Ah, yeah." I felt my cheeks flush. This was merely business, right? I gave him my cell phone number.

"I'll text you so you can put mine on your phone. I'm Adam Harjo."

My random encounter with Adam made me feel better as I drove home. I put out of my mind the possibility that he could be interested in me for any other reasons besides networking. I definitely looked more slovenly than usual, which put me at a new low. But he still wanted to connect.

We were in the same boat: our businesses were basically shuttered. I wasn't as alone as I'd thought I was. I knew the pandemic wasn't about me, but sometimes I felt it was. Everyone else seemed to be successfully "pivoting" into something else. I was trying to move, but why did I feel like I wasn't going anywhere?

I thought about Yumi and the contents of her suitcase. Judging from all the clothes, she'd planned to stay in Kaua'i for a while, and the fact that the Airbnb seemed to be booked for a month supported that. Was she escaping from Japan until tourism opened up? Was she attempting to forge some clandestine deals with tourist spots to sneak in Japanese visitors? I was curious about those Google searches in Japanese. I couldn't read Japanese, but I knew who could.

Sophie and Baachan were slumped on Baachan's sofa bed in her bedroom, watching the latest episode of *Zatoichi*, the blind samurai, on our Panasonic TV, which was literally older than me. Sophie was scrolling through her cell phone, while Baachan's eyes were practically closed.

"Where's Ro?" I asked. I still needed to keep tabs on her.

"She's out in the tent," Sophie reported, keeping her gaze on her phone screen.

"Okay, I need your folks' help."

Chapter Seven

BAACHAN TURNED OFF HER KIKU-TV television program, and Sophie and I sat cross-legged on the bamboo floor. I had to negotiate with Sophie to secure her Japanese-language abilities, promising to take her driving this Saturday.

Sophie stared at the photos that I had taken on my phone for a quick minute.

"It's a search for a law firm," Sophie said.

"Your Japanese is pretty good." I was impressed.

"It says right there in English—Garvin Washburne Law Firm."

"Oh."

Baachan started cackling, her top dentures falling down half an inch. She then closed her mouth, and her prune face became more serious. "I hear of dat Washburne before."

"Yah, right." Baachan often said that she knew everyone who lived on the island, even folks who had never stepped foot below Lihu'e.

"What dis for, anyhow?" Sophie finally looked at my face. "You know you can also use Google Translate for conversations."

"Never mind." I left the dynamic duo in Baachan's bedroom and heard the guttural voice of Zatoichi emanating from the TV again.

Finding my laptop, I googled that lawyer's name. He had recently been in the news in Hawai'i—representing some of the hotels and Airbnb properties that were challenging the quarantine rules for visitors. He also was defending some individuals who had been arrested for breaking quarantine.

The most recent story was that he was representing a fraternity from California, Zeta Alpha Pi, that had been conducting some of its hazing rituals at an Airbnb in Hanalei. Why did those frat boys come all the way to Kaua'i to engage in such nonsense? Just this week, regular protests had been staged outside the rental. In one story, I saw that an activist named Pono had been quoted. I'd met him about a year and a half ago at a protest at a hotel.

"We plan to be here every night until the frat guys are gone," Pono asserted in the story.

It had been more than a year since I had interacted with Pono, but I still had his number in my phone.

I texted: *Hey, P. Leilani Santiago here. Long time no see. Can you give me the address for tonite's protest?*

I waited for a minute. No return text. No matter. I had to take a chance, and got ready to drive back to Hanalei.

One thing I could say about the pandemic: it was making commutes a lot faster. As I zoomed up the highway, I imagined what it would be like if it was clear like this every day. Going back and forth to the North Shore would be no biggie. The only thing was that all this driving was eating up gas. For the first six months of the pandemic, I had only filled up my tank one time, while in this one day I had to pour forty dollars' worth into the Fiesta. I didn't know how I was going to pay off the growing balance on my credit card, but no sense in worrying about it now.

I had already texted Uncle Rick that I was going to stop by his house, and he offered to put me up on his couch in the living room.

Pekelo be happy to see u

Yeah, right, I thought. That text from Uncle Rick just proved how much he didn't know about the dynamics between the Santiago sisters and the Kahuakai brothers.

My okole was sore as I drove into Rick's narrow driveway. His small house always made me smile. It used to be painted a bright yellow, but the color had faded over time. Still, the colors of the surrounding hills and plants—the different shades of green and the red hibiscus—seemed to embrace the home as if the land had integrated it into its landscape.

As I got out of the Ford, I heard a low buzz coming from above. Another drone in the sky.

"Those things are more plenty than the chickens."

Rick was seated in a rattan chair on the porch with his ever-loyal black Labrador, Duke, beside his side.

"And you got a lot of chickens." I could already hear them clucking in the back.

I pulled on a mask before retrieving some dog treats that I'd brought for Duke.

"Hi, boy." Duke's tongue was rough and wet on my palm as he devoured the vegan biscuits that a woman in Waimea made.

Rick frowned as he studied my masked face. "Don't have to wear that—"

"Uncle Rick, you old. If I got you sick, Dad would kill me."

"Okay, you gotta do what you gotta do."

I made sure that I sat at a distance from Rick on the stairs. This had to be one of the best places on the Chen property.

"You want water?" Rick asked.

"Have my water bottle in the car. But I'll have to use your bathroom soon."

"Sure."

"You and Pekelo getting along?"

"He pretty quiet. Except when Emily come around. Then he's talkin' nonstop." Rick petted Duke's shiny coat. "So, whatchu doing on the North Shore?"

"Dakine."

"Whaddaya mean, dakine?"

"Research."

"Planning another Santiago's up here?"

"You lolo, Uncle? We can't even make it down in Waimea."

"One day at a time." Rick subscribed to AA's mantra, but I resented his putting that on me. I could clearly see the future, and it didn't look good.

A weathered pickup truck pulled into the driveway behind the Ford. Pekelo jumped out from the driver's seat. He was wearing a sleeveless shirt stained with mud and probably sweat, judging from the smell. His cargo pants and calves were also muddy.

"Howzit," Pekelo greeted me. He searched the porch. "Is Em here?"

"No, just me. Sorry."

Pekelo switched gears, but the disappointment remained on his face. "Always good to see you."

"Bulai."

"I no lie. I'm going to take a quick shower."

"Wait, let me go shi-shi first." I ran in and did my business.

After I came out, the whole crew, including Duke, was back in the house.

"There's chili in the crockpot. You two can eat." Rick stirred the contents of his slow cooker on the kitchen table. Onolicious smell. I had to get his recipe.

I went into the kitchen to get a bowlful of freshly steamed rice and spooned the chili over it. It had been so long since I ate someone else's hot cooking, and I relished every morsel.

"Hey, slow down." Pekelo came out of the shower, a towel hanging from his neck to capture the moisture from the long, wet curls on his head.

"Uncle, dis broke da mouth!" I gave Rick my ultimate compliment. "Onolicious."

Pekelo went into the kitchen to get himself a bowl of gohan and began to chow down his chili and rice.

"Looks like you two are competing in a chili-eating contest," Rick said, looking proud of himself.

As I finished the last of my food, my phone dinged. A text from Pono with the address of the protest location.

"Oh, have to go."

"Hot date?" Rick asked. He asked that one like it was a joke.

Even Pekelo had a toothy grin.

"No. There's a protest at that Airbnb where those frat boys are staying."

"Why you like go ova dere?" While probably sympathetic to Pono's group's point of view, Pekelo wasn't that political.

"There's a lawyer that I'm looking into. Garvin Washburne. Heard of him?"

Both Pekelo and Rick shook their heads.

"Ah, Pekelo, can you move your truck? You're blocking me in."

"I betta go wid you." Pekelo quickly chewed the last of his meal.

"I can take care of myself."

"Yah, heard that before."

"Go with her," Rick added his two cents. He looked concerned, and I didn't want to cause him any undue stress. After we got into Pekelo's truck, I plugged in the house address to Google Maps for Pekelo to follow. The ride in his pickup was rough; I think it needed some new shock absorbers.

"So, I heard you gave some Japanese lady some mouth to mouth." Pekelo took a cigarette from a package held in place by the truck's visor. He offered me one, but I shook my head. While I was dying for one, I had stopped smoking about a year ago.

"What was I supposed to do? Let her die?"

"Yeah, most would." Pekelo was having a hard time lighting his cigarette as he bounced in the driver's seat. "She's a tour agent, right? Why she ova here during a pandemic?"

I shook my head. "I dunno. Dat's why I'm here. To figure it out."

"Don't you have anyting bettah to do?" Pekelo blew out some cigarette smoke.

I gave him stink eye and he got quiet. There was practically nothing better for me to do right now, and he knew it too.

I attempted to change the subject. "So, how's work?"

"Cutting kalo? Honest work. To be out there with my machete. All my anger just comes out. You should try sometimes."

"Do I seem angry?"

"Just hear tings."

Since I had hardly interacted with Pekelo during the early months of the pandemic, this observation had to come from only one source: Emily. I wanted to probe him further about his relationship with her, but I also wanted to ensure that I had a ride back to Uncle Rick's.

When we got a few blocks away from our destination, we saw a line of cars parked by the side of the road. "Park if you see anything open," I told Pekelo. The word was out about the protest, and I could see people standing in the street.

Pekelo made a U-turn and found a spot beside a row of short palm trees. The foliage here was thick and green. There was no need for walls or fences. Man just tamed bushes and other plants for privacy.

I adjusted my mask over my face, and Pekelo did the same with a black one he had hanging from his rearview mirror. As soon as I jumped out of the truck, I felt the moisture from the ocean air coat my bare arms and legs. It was too dark to clearly see the waterline, but I could hear the crash of waves in the distance.

The protesters seemed like a random, eclectic group. I spotted older aunties, probably kānaka maoli, who were leading the group in chants.

A few feet away from the aunties was Pono, wearing a mask featuring the native Hawaiian flag in red, gold, and green.

"Hey, howzit?" he greeted Pekelo first. Normally, the two men would have put their foreheads together and breathed life into each other, a proper Hawaiian greeting among warriors. But COVID-19 had put a stop to such traditional greetings.

Instead, they bumped fists. Awkward. With me, Pono extended an elbow. Even more awkward. "Leilani. Good to see you, sistah." He gestured toward Pekelo. "I didn't know you knew each oddah."

"We grew up with each oddah in Waimea," I explained. "Practically braddah and sistah."

Pekelo didn't look happy with my description. I knew what was going on in his mind. If we were practically family, was his relationship with Emily crossing a line? He tried to change the subject. "Those Mainland college boys in dere?"

Pono nodded. "We'll smoke dem out. Eventually. Those aunties are leading the way."

It was good to see Pono take a back seat in the protests. I had seen him get eviscerated by all sides because of his high profile in Kaua'i's controversies about native lands in the last few years. He must have received the message, because he was definitely letting the older women call the shots.

A patrol car came around the corner, and I felt the tension level of the crowd heighten. The chatter became louder, and gestures became more exaggerated. My own body felt tense, on full alert.

"Here we go," Pono said.

Out of the parked black-and-white emerged Andy and my nemesis and distant relative, Chief Dennis Toma.

The chief scanned the crowd, and then his gaze stopped at me. Of all the people he would approach, it would have to be me.

"You a ways from Waimea, Santiago," Toma said.

"Free country, as far as I heard," I said back to him.

Both Pono and Pekelo stood still and silent, but I figured they were enjoying this show.

"Chief Toma," Andy called out, quite conveniently. He didn't bother to acknowledge me, which was best for both of us. Toma quickly made his way back to Andy and a couple of the aunties he was talking to.

I exhaled and noticed that Pono seemed to give me more respect for having given Chief Toma some attitude. Little did he know that Toma and I were blood relatives. That information I was going to keep to myself.

More people had arrived, and I studied the various individuals on the outskirts of the circle. I knew what Garvin Washburne looked like from his website, and there was no sign of him in this crowd. I knew lawyer types usually worked behind the scenes, but then this was Kaua'i, and it wouldn't be unusual for someone like Washburne to appear at a protest.

I did recognize one haole man. "That guy looks familiar," I said.

"Who?" Pono asked.

"The haole guy ova there."

Pono craned his head to where I gestured.

"Oh, Ted."

"Yah, that's what I thought. He's a nurse."

"He's been coming out. He lives out in Hanalei."

"He does? He works ova in Waimea. Why would he work so far if he lives up here?"

Pono shrugged. "You know these haoles. Probably came for the North Shore. He's from somewhere in the South. Tennessee, or something like that."

Before Pono or Pekelo could say anything more, I made my way toward Ted, who was standing by himself in a black mask. He seemed content to be isolated and away from everyone else.

"Hello. Ted, right?"

Ted looked startled that I knew his name.

"I'm Sammie's friend. Leilani Santiago. You gave me my COVID test the other day."

"Oh." His forehead relaxed a little.

"I tested negative, so don't worry."

Ted was obviously not the joking type.

"You interested in shutting down this Airbnb?"

He shrugged his shoulders.

A red razorback hog was in the center of his mask. I recognized the logo. During my college volleyball days, we'd played the University of Arkansas once in a tournament. "The Razorbacks," I commented.

"What?"

I repeated myself. "Razorbacks. You from Arkansas?"

Ted didn't reply. Seemed like he hadn't yet adopted the aloha spirit. This was a most awkward conversation, and I was happy to see a familiar figure joining Pono and Pekelo, a notebook in her hand. I excused myself from Ted, not that he would have missed me.

"You're sure getting around the island," Taylor commented as I walked toward the group.

"You too."

"Well, this is *my* job."

"I thought Pablo Sanchez was covering the protests."

"He's working on a writeup about a couple that came back from visiting California with a positive COVID test."

"That happens, right?"

"But they knew it. They are from Kaua'i. They had their kids with them. DCFS took away their kids at the airport."

For a second I felt sorry for the couple. They shouldn't have brought the virus with them to the island, but I could empathize with their desperation. They wanted to get home

by any means necessary. But they'd made a very bad calcu-
lation, which then led to what they surely wanted to avoid
in the first place: family separation.

I took another look for Washburne. Behind us was an
older haole woman with a hollowed-out neck who stood a
distance from everyone else.

"Who's dat?" I asked Pono.

He turned his head. "She's the wife of the frat boys'
attorney."

Interesting. "Why she here?"

"Some folks thought she was a spy, but it turns out that
she hates him. He got himself a mistress about half his age.
He's hiding out in his rental right down the street, the house
with the Japanese roof. Won't come out. I guess the wife's
hoping he'll show up, one of these days."

"So he neva shows up? Even though he's representing
the fraternity?" I was disappointed.

"Why you care?" Pekelo interjected, correctly smelling
that I had ulterior motives in coming to Hanalei.

"Just wondering."

"Eh, Pono," an auntie in a batik sarong called out, and
Pono, receiving permission to get involved, excused himself
to talk to the elders.

Another car arrived on the scene and double-parked
in the middle of the road. I thought the police would move
the driver along, but it was the mayor! I was thinking of
snapping a photo, but Sophie would feel so bad to be miss-
ing out. He consulted with Chief Toma for a few minutes,
and the two of them made their way to the doorway of
the house.

All the protesters hushed as the door opened and a
young blond man stepped out to talk to the police.

"These Mainland haoles," Pekelo said. He'd brought his cigarettes and was lighting another one. "I wish they just stayed where they came from."

"They not all bad."

"Talkin' about Sean, eh?" Pekelo almost sneered. He was definitely not a fan of Waimea Junction's landlord. Pekelo was perfectly happy not to be working part-time at my father's surf shop, Killer Wave, in the Junction.

"He's forgiven our rent for six months. We'd be sunk without that. And he's trying to bring high-tech to Kaua'i."

"Sure." There was no convincing Pekelo of Sean's merits.

I didn't want to argue about this. Sean didn't need me to defend him, anyway.

The crowd, meanwhile, seemed more relaxed now that the mayor had arrived. I felt like I was at a tailgate for a University of Hawai'i football game—not a protest concerning island self-determination.

I hoped people wouldn't be disappointed with the results of the negotiation.

After about half an hour, the mayor and Chief Toma emerged from the house and made their way down the landscaped walkway. I braced myself for the news.

Taylor was out front, taking video with her iPhone.

The mayor kept his mask on as he delivered his update to the crowd. "I'm charged with keeping Kaua'i safe and will continue to do so," he said. "The renters of this Airbnb have announced that they will be going home tomorrow. We will be escorting them to the airport first thing in the morning."

The crowd expressed their approvals with applause and masked cheers. Both Pekelo and I were surprised. We didn't expect that these unwanted visitors would clear out so quickly. They had probably been blindsided by this passionate organic pushback, however disorganized it was.

I searched the back for Washburne's wife and then Ted, but both were gone.

Before we left, Pekelo checked the bed of the truck. "Dammit, I thought my machete was in here."

"What, you tink someone wen take'um?"

"Eh, maybe I left it at work. My head not working so good. Pandemic brain."

"You probably still hungry." I was starting to feel bad about interrupting Pekelo's evening meal.

As we drove back to Rick's, I texted Mom and Emily to tell them I'd be spending the night in Hanalei. I expected an immediate text back from Emily, at least, but got no response from either of them.

It was dark now, and the mountains loomed like dinosaurs in front of us. But it wasn't frightening. More like ancient protective friends.

It felt liberating to have a change of scenery. It was wetter on the North Shore, and I felt bathed and revitalized by the moisture.

"Come to Waimea sometime. Court and Kelly miss you," I said, not really knowing whether they did or not.

"I've been talkin' to Kelly."

"You have?"

"You know what's going on with him and Court?"

I was shocked into silence. I was unaware of any problems.

"You know dat Lee's Flowers may have to close down."

"No, Court nevah say notting to me."

"Court's parents are keeping it quiet. Dey no like Court for worry too much right now."

"But dat's not right." As Lee's Flowers' successor, Court should know what was going on with the family business.

"I told Kelly I can get him one job ova here. At least temporary."

"In the fields?"

"Someting wrong with dat?"

"No, notting." Pekelo, a former Navy man, had defined, sinewy muscles on his arms, chest, and legs. Kelly, on the other hand, was like the rest of us: he was getting a bit soft around the middle and face. His pandemic body wasn't prepared for manual labor.

"But Court has no idea of any of dis. You no tink she should know?"

"Court knows more than she lets on. She pretends that she's a nice girl, but she not that nice a girl."

My mouth dropped open. Pekelo was talking about my BFF, someone I had known all my life. "Court like a sistah to me."

"I got to know Court since she and Kūheakapu got married. If she no get her way, she can be mento. She throws things, you know."

"Nah."

"You know her as a friend, Leilani. Dat different than in a marriage relationship. You still have a lot to learn."

Whatthehell? "Don't need no lecture from you about relationships," I snapped at him, and I stayed quiet during the rest of the ride home. I didn't need to hear the truth from Pekelo. It hurt too much.

Pekelo sensed that I was mad and was smart enough to keep his mouth shut too. Before he pulled into the driveway, I told him I wanted to pull my car out onto the street. He waited as I jumped out and backed the Fiesta out. By the time I returned inside, he had disappeared into his room. Good riddance.

Both Pekelo and I had been in Court and Kelly's wedding. The ceremony wasn't the type that tourists had in boats floating in front of the majestic Na Pali Mountains or on the green lawns of the plantation resorts. No, their wedding was at their church in Hanapepe, filled with people whom they both knew and didn't know that well. Court was a vision, a real-life angel in tulle and lace. She almost seemed to be floating down the aisle with Mr. Lee, all cleaned up in a suit and tie and his hair combed back like a mafia boss. I was forced to wear a yellow cocktail dress that made me feel like Big Bird next to the delicate Court. Baachan made it a point to find me several times during the reception and laugh. I had definitely made her night.

Our high school classmates kept warning Court to expect that something would go wrong—those bitches— but nothing did. It had rained a little the night before, seen as a blessing; and sure enough, the sun broke out the morning of the wedding, even gifting the couple with a rainbow. Photo op! Most people showed up on time, except for Mr. Lee's distant cousin from O'ahu—no one liked her much anyway, so it turned out to be for the best.

The reception was mostly potluck, and it seemed that all the aunties were competing to produce the best musubis, potato salad, butter mochi, and homemade kimchi. Pekelo changed from his suit to his trademark tank top, camouflage cargo pants, and slippah to oversee the barbecuing of kalbi ribs and teriyaki chicken. Soon the smell of smoke overpowered the stephanotis and freesia in our bouquets. I had to keep my dress on, but I replaced my platform shoes with my Crocs. It was a perfect day.

I never dreamt of weddings like Court did. Thinking about people staring at me walking down the aisle in a white dress gives me chicken skin. Aside from the ceremony, though, having a life partner holds its allure. To have someone next to me in bed, holding me tight every night, was something I very much wanted. To hear that Court and Kelly, the ideal couple in my life, might be having problems disturbed me to my core. If they couldn't make it work, who in the world could?

Thursday

Chapter Eight

THE NEXT MORNING, I pulled myself off Rick's couch, which was way too soft for my back. It was seven, and the house was quiet and still, aside from the chickens squawking outside.

I was glad not to encounter Pekelo. His cynical words had cut into me last night. I knew I was inexperienced with relationships, especially of the romantic kind. At the beginning of the year I was getting to know a sales rep with a Big Island–based coffee company, but of course my contact with him had virtually ended by the beginning of April. I occasionally lurked on his Instagram account, where he continued to feature specials for their coffees. Unlike shave ice, there was still a demand for coffee, especially through mail order and grocery stores. One of his IG posts included a playful selfie with one of his coworkers, a young Asian woman with straight bangs across her forehead. I went to her account, but it was set to private. Her daily life was closed to me, ending my sleuthing into their relationship.

I found one of those free scratch paper notebooks from a local realtor and quickly wrote a note for Uncle Rick.

Uncle—
Mahalo for everything.
Stay safe. And say hello to Auntie Barbara for me.
Love, Leilani

I placed the note in the middle of the kitchen table. Pekelo, on the other hand, didn't deserve any thanks from me.

I checked my phone, and there was only a text from my mom:

Glad you getting a quick getaway. No hurry. We can take care of things while you are away.

Rather than making me feel better, Mom's text made me feel even more useless. Nobody needed me in Waimea. Boo-hoo. Pity party. Yeah, I was getting pretty good about feeling sorry for myself.

Before I left, I quickly washed my face in the bathroom, checking on the pimples that had sprouted on my forehead and chin. Here I was, twenty-five years old and dealing with acne again. I wasn't sure if it was related to so much mask-wearing or stress. Or maybe a little of both.

I was happy that I'd moved my car onto the street last night so I didn't have to wake Pekelo to move his truck. The less I had to deal with him, the better. I clicked on Google Maps, and there was my last destination, the neighborhood of the ZAP boys. Down that street was the attorney's house. I hated that I'd spent all this time to come up here and I was returning with nothing. What if I knocked on the attorney's door? Made up a lie that Yumi had been a business acquaintance and I needed to get in touch with her family. He'd probably slam the door in my face. But I was here, and I could deal with rejection. Especially from a haole man whom I didn't know.

As I drove onto Alealea Road, everything seemed quiet. There was some rubbish strewn in the middle of the street. Clear disposable takeout drink cups and someone's rubbah slippahs. Protesters could be trash, literal litterbugs.

The frat boys' rental cars were still parked in the driveway, so they hadn't left yet. And no sign of any police escorts.
In the light of early morning, I could more clearly make out
the house and see the outline of the sea only a few yards
away. The building was made of light wood, reminding me
of a tropical cabin in paradise. The sloping hills in the background were a rich, vibrant green.

I drove half a block down to the house that the attorney
was supposedly renting. The homes here were more well-
kept. The lawyer's rental was a small ranch house with a
Japanese tile roof and a neat lawn.

I parked on the street, noticing at least one other car
out front. In the driveway was a Lexus with the license plate
WASHATTY1. Had to be his car. I heard something up in
the distance and expected one of the North Shore's alba-
trosses, but instead it was a lone light blue drone. What the
heck. Super-annoying.

I went up the stone pathway and hesitated for a
moment. What was I thinking? But then I recalled the air
that I'd blown into Yumi's body. She had survived the waves
of Waimea Bay. She needed to be embraced by those who
loved her.

I stood on the porch of the house, which was painted
gray.

I was getting ready to ring the doorbell when I heard
a *bang!*, which sounded like a gunshot coming from inside
the house. I froze for a moment. Was my own life in danger?
The shattering of glass from the back of the house jerked me
into action. I ran to the Ford and somehow, in spite of my
hands shaking, was able to force my keys into the ignition
and drive forward a few yards. I stopped in front of the frat
house and punched in 911. I could barely get the words out

after a female voice identified herself. "I heard a gunshot at a house in Waimea."

"What is the location?" the dispatcher asked.

There were no street signs, so I referred back to my phone for the intersection.

"What is your name?" she said.

"Leilani Santiago."

The dispatcher paused for a moment, and I wondered if my bad reputation—and my father's—had preceded me.

"And where are you?"

"I'm in a turquoise blue Ford Fiesta at the intersection."

"I'm sending a unit to you."

I sat in the car, my palms sweaty around the steering wheel.

It hurt to breathe, and I wondered if I'd contracted COVID after taking the test on Sunday.

Was this trouble related to last night's protest? The frat boys had agreed to leave, so why would anyone have a beef with their lawyer? Unless one of the college students was unhappy with Garvin's legal representation. He certainly had opted to be in the background of the controversy.

Within five minutes, a bevy of patrol cars, their sirens blaring, came around the corner and passed me on their way to the attorney's rental.

Uh, hello. I'm over here, I thought. I turned my head, confused about what was going on. Sure, I'd reported what I thought was a gunshot and possible break-in, but this response seemed like overkill.

The uniformed officers converged on the ranch house, while one of the officers peered down the street and started walking toward me. I put on a mask and got out of the car.

"You Leilani Santiago?" he asked when he was about six feet away.

I nodded.

He took a notebook from his pocket. "I need to know exactly what you saw. First of all, why are you here?"

It would be too much to go into how I had helped save Yumi Hara's life. And my current obsession with helping her would certainly cast doubt on my mental health. I instead said, "I wanted to talk to the attorney, Garvin Washburne."

"Had you met him before?"

I shook my head. "But I was at the protest last night, and folks told me he lived over in that house. I needed to talk to him. About a legal matter." That was weak, because obviously Washburne's work number was listed on his website. There was no need for me to pay him a house visit. Why was I here at eight o'clock in the morning to bother a stranger?

The officer's dark brown eyes over his mask didn't reveal any emotion. Who knows what he was really thinking?

"Wait here," he ordered and walked back to his parked black-and-white.

Another siren rang out, and an ambulance turned onto the street and raced to the attorney's house.

Was Garvin shot? And here I was on his doorstep with a weak reason to be on the premises of a crime scene. *Leilani, you got lousy timing*, I said to myself.

I wanted to reach out to someone for help, but who could that be? Everyone around me was burdened by their own problems. I was feeling so desperate that I even considered calling Dad. But I imagined him in the middle of making some deal with ABC. If I somehow hurt his chances for some financial success, which our family depended on, I'd never forgive myself.

Since I had no options, I returned to the driver's seat, biting the edge of my thumb like Sophie was prone to do.

The fraternity boys had started to emerge from the Airbnb with suitcases in hand. They stuffed their luggage into the trunks of their rental cars. A couple of them noticed the hubbub down the street, and one of them saw that I was sitting in the Ford, watching everything unfold.

One of them was thin, with brown hair, reminding me a little of my ex-boyfriend in Seattle. He didn't look like the stereotypical frat boys I saw in movies. There were of course fraternities and sororities at UW, but I hadn't been there long enough to differentiate the various types of members. I was fixated on my academic survival, and unfortunately it didn't go my way.

This one came close to the Ford and waved his hands to get my attention. "What's going on?" he asked through my open window.

"Something happened at the house where Garvin Washburne lives."

"Really?"

He ran back to his friends, and they huddled together as if they were trying to figure out their next move.

While they were conferring, the patrol officer found me again. "You'll have to come to police headquarters in Līhuʻe."

"How come?"

"Chief is insisting on it."

"Chief Toma knows that I'm here?"

"You the one who reported the crime."

But what crime? I was almost too scared to ask. "What's going on? Did something happen to Mr. Washburne?"

The officer again ignored my question. It looked like nothing had changed with my relationship with the island police.

"You need the address to police headquarters?"

"No, I know it." Only too well.

Before I started the car, I found Emily's name on my phone and started writing her a text.

I may be in trouble. Can u meet me at Līhu'e police HQ?

This time her reply was immediate: *What happened?*

No time to get into it now. Can u go and come?

She immediately sent me the thumbs-up icon.

I got on the highway, driving a bit emotionally and crossing the lines on the road. How ironic would it be if I was pulled over by the police on my way over to the headquarters?

After I passed Princeville, my phone dinged with a text. It was Emily. *Court and I are on our way.*

Court? Why did Emily have to involve Court? But then I realized that I had our only wheels. She had no choice but to ask Court for the van, and, knowing Court, she wasn't going to let Emily go alone.

As I was driving through Kapa'a, I received another text. Emily again. *We're here.*

At a stoplight, I hurriedly replied back. *Wait in parking lot. B there in 15.*

When I turned into the practically empty police lot, I immediately saw Court's minivan parked by the entrance. I grabbed a spot next to them.

Emily emerged from the passenger side while Court stayed in the driver's seat with her window rolled down.

"What happened?" There were sleep marks from bed-sheets on Emily's face, so I knew I had woken her up.

"Something happened at the house where Garvin Washburne was staying. I was at his door when I heard something like a gunshot coming from his house."

"Washburne? What were you doing with him?" Emily asked.

"You know him?"

"He's well known in legal circles in Hawai'i. He was with a big law firm in Honolulu. I heard that he recently moved full-time to Kaua'i, and I was hoping to run into him for a possible internship."

I wished I'd known that Emily was so well acquainted with Washburne. Her information might have saved me a whole hell of a lot of time.

"How do you know him?" she asked me.

"Well, I don't. The woman we pulled out of Waimea Bay—her name is Yumi Hara. She's connected to him in some way."

Court must have been listening to us the whole time. "Is that why you went to Hanalei?" She leaned out the window, as much as her big belly would allow.

"I want to help her. She's got no one here."

Court sat back in the driver's seat, her skinny arms folded on the steering wheel. She obviously didn't get my obsession with Yumi. Truth be told, I didn't get it either. I usually was too overwhelmed with my own problems to be concerned with anyone else's. But in the pandemic, my problems had become long and insurmountable. I couldn't address them until the roar of the virus passed us by.

"I was doing this all for you and Kelly, Court," I explained. "To find out what Yumi was doing here in Kaua'i, making trouble for all of us, especially your parents." And also to help her get home to Japan. But I didn't share that part with Emily and Court, because they probably wouldn't believe that I had gone so soft.

"Just forget about her, Leilani. My parents worry too much."

I thought about what Pekelo had said about the family flower business. Judging by the strange expression on Em's face, he'd shared the same story with her too.

"Well, let's just deal with what's at hand." Emily had found the lawyer in her. "Stay in the van, Court. I'll go in with Leilani."

After masking up, we entered the lobby, and I gave my name to the receptionist at the window. Emily and I then waited on a wooden bench.

"Haven't been inside here for years," Emily said.

My father and I, on the other hand, were much better acquainted with the police facilities, especially the jail. "Wish I could say the same," I said.

Emily frowned for a moment. "Oh, the trouble that you and Dad got in last year. The surfer boy from Los Angeles, right?"

"He was from the OC." In the big scheme of things, it was such a minor detail, but it was satisfying to correct Em. The surfer's death had rocked our circle in Kaua'i, and I couldn't believe that Emily was speaking about it so casually.

"The attorney that I found for Dad really helped out, huh?" She was remembering a detail that I'd forgotten. I was annoyed again, feeling annoyed that I felt annoyed. Emily wasn't saying any of this to assert her significance. It was just her way to feel connected to us while she was in California in law school. But I couldn't help but be put back in my place—a college dropout who'd failed to make it on the Mainland.

Chief Toma appeared around the corner. Last night at the protest, the sun was going down and I didn't notice all the gray in Toma's hair. He hadn't had so much last year. The promotion and the pandemic seemed to be taking a toll on him.

"You can't stay away from trouble, can you, Leilani?" he said, directing me to follow him into one of the conference rooms.

Emily, of course, was right by my side, causing Toma to abruptly stop walking. "What's this?"

"I'm her representative."

"Have you even finished law school yet?" Even though Chief Toma didn't even acknowledge Emily by name, he obviously knew all about her.

"I didn't say I was her legal representative. I'm her sister. And I want to be with her. Are you charging her with anything?"

Toma sighed. "Just come in, then."

Each of us masked, we sat in the conference room, which was a nice word for an interrogation room. Emily and I sat on chairs that were positioned several feet away from the table, which made me feel like I was back in the high school principal's office. Toma put a yellow notepad on the table, and I felt my blood pressure rise. My earlier irritation with my golden sister, Emily, disappeared. I was so happy to have her by my side.

Toma dove in fast. "What were you doing at Garvin Washburne's house?"

"Shouldn't you first tell us why you've brought Leilani in?" Emily was ready to fight for me.

"Look, I just want to get some clarification. Leilani isn't a person of interest. At least not now."

What the hell did that mean? If that was supposed to help me open up, it wasn't working.

I glanced at Emily, and she nodded for me to speak. "I wanted to ask him some questions."

"About what?"

"Yumi Hara. The woman that my sisters and I saved from the ocean in Waimea."

"How did you know they were connected?" I could imagine Chief Toma's frown even through his mask.

"So they are?" I couldn't say that I'd broken into her Airbnb and found the Google printouts listing his information.

"Well, just tell me what happened this morning." Toma seemed willing to drop how I'd come to find out about Yumi and Garvin.

I repeated the story I'd told the patrol officer: I was standing on his doorstep when I heard the gunshot and then glass breaking. Toma's black pen moved swiftly on his notepad. You'd think the Kaua'i Police Department would join the twenty-first century and input notes in a phone or laptop instead.

"Wait a minute." Toma stopped writing. "In that order? It's very important that you be precise."

"Yah, one gunshot, and then maybe three seconds later someting shattering inside."

"Why? What happened in there?" Emily asked. Her phone began dinging, once, twice, and a third time.

Super-annoying, I said to myself, and Chief Toma seemed to agree.

Noticing the chief's dirty looks, Emily stood up. "I have to leave for a sec."

No, Em, don't leave me, I thought, but tried to cover up my desperation. Showing any kind of weakness in front of Chief Toma would be fatal.

As soon as Emily disappeared out the door, Toma circled back to Yumi Hara.

"I'm still curious why you think Yumi and the lawyer are connected."

"Well, she works for a large Japanese tour company, right?" My mind went back to Taylor's articles. What details were public knowledge? For one thing, she'd defied quarantine when she'd first arrived. "And didn't Washburne end up representing her when she left her hotel?"

"No, he didn't, but Miss Hara did contact him while she was in Kaua'i. We have phone records that reveal that, but I wonder how you would know."

"Lucky guess?"

"I don't believe in luck and I don't believe in guesses."

"Well, regarding this morning, I can't keep repeating the same thing over and over. I heard what I heard."

Toma finally put down his pen. "Okay. You can go. But don't go far."

I didn't think Chief Toma was much of a joker, but that was funny. Where could I go in a pandemic? On a small island?

I walked out of the conference room into the wide hallway. *Free at last!* I attempted to strut, as much as I could in my Crocs, only to spy Emily with Pekelo by the front door.

"What you doin' here?" Was Pekelo that attached to Emily that he couldn't be away from her for forty-eight hours?

"Got called in by police." Pekelo didn't seem happy to be at the station.

"Why?"

"They found my machete in dat lawyer's house."

"What?" This made no sense.

"It's Sammie's coworker, the nurse." Emily shared what the police revealed to Pekelo. "I think his name is Ted. Ted broke into Washburne's house with the machete, and the lawyer shot him dead."

Friday

Chapter Nine

THE NEXT DAY, the story was in all the island newspapers and even KHON-TV news in Honolulu. It made for a great promo: Crazed nurse participating in an anti-tourism rally attacks a respected attorney with a machete and is gunned to death.

A group of us early-morning Santiagos crowded in Baachan's back room to watch the news together. A masked reporter with sprayed hair was standing in front of Garvin Washburne's rented house. The TV camera panned over to the ocean. "The nurse came to Kaua'i right before the pandemic," the reporter said. "Mr. Washburne has no idea why Ted Rumpf broke into his home with intent to harm him. Mr. Washburne did not want to be interviewed on camera but said there were many hateful and threatening comments posted about him on social media regarding his support for opening up tourism in Hawai'i."

"Did you see the gun, Leilani?" Dani's voice sounded muffled as she sucked on a strand of her wavy hair.

"No, notting like that. I didn't even know what happened inside."

Sophie seemed in awe of me for being in the presence of island-wide news, and was quiet.

Baachan was the only one to pooh-pooh the incident. "These haoles come ova from the Mainland and go lolo. Why not just stay in Kansas and make trouble there?"

"Baachan, he was from Arkansas. Totally different place."

"Kansas, Ar-Kansas, it's all the same to me."

"Baachan, you know how silly you sound. How about people on the Mainland who don't know that Hawai'i is part of the United States?"

"Well, they are just bakatare." Baachan declared that they were stupid, and both Dani and Sophie tittered to hear our grandmother curse in Japanese.

"You bakatare," Sophie said to Dani, pressing her toes into our youngest sister's calves.

"No, *you* bakatare." Dani spit out the hair from her mouth. Oh, another day in paradise.

I rose, but before I could leave the room Sophie called out to me: "No forget, you promised to take me driving tomorrow."

I *had* forgotten. The last thing I wanted was to spend a couple of hours alone with her, but she had helped me earlier with the Japanese translation, so I needed to be more generous.

I went outside to give Jimin some feed and check in with Ro. Even though I told her to stay in the girls' bedroom at night, she'd slept outside in the tent. The nights had been warm—even for us in Waimea—so at least I didn't have to worry that she'd catch a cold.

I shook the outside of the tent and bent down toward the zippered front. "Hey, Ro. You up?"

Ro was reading one of Sophie's manga books while lying in my sleeping bag. I was now sleeping on a foam egg crate covered with a sheet. My back was taking a beating and was almost feeling sore enough for one of Baachan's killer massages. They were killer because you felt like you were dying while she dug her elbows and calloused palms into your back. A few minutes later, however, you lost all feeling, including pain. It would last at least a day.

"Come inside and eat some cereal. We're all going to Waimea Junction to use the Wi-Fi there."

Ro put the book down and sat up. "Okay," she said.

Ro was so much easier to deal with than Sophie. I knew it was because she was a little on edge, being in somebody else's house. But she nonetheless was a good influence on my little sister, and I didn't mind her being around.

I went into the kitchen and got out four bowls. I poured the generic Cheerios into each, and then a healthy splash of milk into three. I only put a little in the fourth and diluted it with tap water. That was mine. They were all growing girls, but I was growing in places where I didn't want to.

"Hey, breakfast," I bellowed and began to eat my cereal standing up at the sink. Through the kitchen window, I could see Jimin, energized by the feed I gave him, strutting through the tall grasses at the side of our house.

I was still processing what I had seen on the news. Was Ted an anti-tourist activist? As far as I knew, he had no close ties to the island. He was from the South—a haole to top all haoles. And why had I heard the gunshot and then the breaking of the glass? None of this added up.

After rinsing out my bowl and spoon, I texted Sammie to see where she was.

She quickly responded. *Andy and I taking care of shopping b4 work.*

I texted an invitation. *Come by Santiago's. Tell Andy I make grape shave ice.*

Since we were running a little late, I drove Sophie, Ro, and Dani down to Waimea Junction. The girls moved the picnic table closer to the building so they could get a good Wi-Fi connection. We ran an extension cord from the shave ice shack so everyone had access to an outlet for their computers. Santiago's, in a strange way, had become more than a place to cool down and slurp shave ice. It had become a school.

The bribe of grape shave ice must have been too much for Andy to resist, because in about an hour his jeep appeared in the parking lot, with Sammie in the passenger seat.

The girls hadn't seen Sammie in a while and abandoned their laptops to say hello.

"Eh, you three still in class," I yelled at them.

Sammie crinkled her forehead above her mask. "You sound like Mrs. Ikkanda," she said, referring to a high school teacher who'd been at our old school, like, forever.

"Mrs. Ikkanda is like seventy years old now."

Sophie lifted her arms, saying if the shoe fits, I'm definitely wearing them.

"Whatchu want, Sammie? Coconut?"

Sammie gave me a thumbs-up and went over to the girls to catch up with them.

After making their ices, I brought them out. Sammie and Andy sat outside Sean's storefront, Books and Suds.

Sammie looked a bit shaky. She had dark circles under her eyes. When she removed her mask to eat her coconut ice, I saw that she was without her trademark hot-pink lip gloss. Her face was naked with grief.

"I hate the way the news is making him out to be," she said about Ted. "I found some good photos that I gave the hospital PR person. But the worst one is on TV. That's from his hospital ID. He looks like a white-supremacist hater."

"What do you know about Ted, anyway?"

Until now, Andy had been focused on his grape ice. Now he jerked his head up. "What are you up to, Leilani?"

"No, I'm just wondering why a guy from Arkansas came all the ways over to Kaua'i. Did he have a girlfriend here or someting?"

Sammie shook her head. "No, I don't think so. I mean, I didn't know him all that well. He came to Hawai'i in the middle of the pandemic, maybe in May. But one time he mentioned that his sister died of COVID. Early on, like in April. He was really broken up over that."

"She must have been pretty young."

"Yeah. I think his hometown was a hotspot. Poultry factory."

"Any other family members?"

"No, it was just him and his sister. Sad story."

It was. My compassion for Ted's situation deepened. I knew nothing about him, but sibling love I understood. Maybe he had come to Kaua'i to get away from his problems? He wouldn't be the first person to do so. But then why attack Washburne?

"Do you know if he knew the lawyer?"

"Leilani!" Andy put his empty cup on the ground.

"What?" I attempted to bat my eyelashes.

"Did someting get in your eye?" Sammie asked, concerned.

"No."

"Leilani just being niele."

"I'm not being nosy. Just smell stink. Yumi Hara in Kaua'i to see Washburne. And then Ted attack him. Is that a coincidence? There's someting between Yumi and Ted."

"But Ted from Kansas and Yumi from Japan."

"Arkansas."

"Huh?"

"Never mind. See, the fact that they so different means there's someting dere."

Sammie tightened her grip on her wooden spoon, contemplating what I'd said.

I turned my attention to Andy, who had put on his mask. "Anyway, you can get photos of Garvin Washburne house?"

"Of a crime scene? No can do. If the boss hear about helpin' you, I'm dead."

"Please, Andy," said Sammie. "Leilani's good at figurin' stuff out."

I was shocked by her comment. That was definitely the nicest thing she'd ever said about me.

Andy must have been in love, because the lines on his forehead disappeared. "I'll see what I can do. But no can promise."

"Mahalo." I felt a tiny bit of stress leave my shoulders. At least there was a possibility of figuring out this mystery. "Hey, by the way, do you two know anyone with a beat-up Honda motorcycle with a jacked muffler?"

Sammie repeated what Court had said—that most of the guys from our high school had a motorcycle somehow in the back of their parents' garage.

Andy was actually able to name a person. "Only Taiji Wong, but he's been out of state during the pandemic." The frown returned, his purple-stained lips making him look like an ancient warrior. "Why?"

I shrugged my shoulders. I knew that I was pushing my luck with Andy, and backed off.

Andy and Sammie finally rose, thanking me for the shave ice and telling me that they had to get going. As I turned to walk them to Andy's jeep, I saw half a dozen other students from Sophie and Ro's school standing around the picnic table.

"Howzit?" I asked, but more with the tone of *what are you guys doing here*.

"The Wi-Fi here is better than at our houses," one of them said. "Can we do some work here?"

The girls looked up at me expectantly, as if I could remedy their friends' problems with a nod of my head.

I granted their request, but with caveats. "You supposed to social-distance. Remembah what Mayor Kawakami was telling you all. Get out the table from the back and bring ova here."

The newcomer teens broke out in smiles, and even Sophie and Dani joined them to help. I went into the shack to find another extension cord. If only the rest of our problems could be solved so easily.

Chapter Ten

I SPENT THE REST OF THE DAY on the internet like the kids. I googled how other shave ice shops were faring during the pandemic. A few on Kaua'i had reopened. More on O'ahu, of course. There were more residents there, and all those resort bubbles. We in Waimea had no fancy hotels, just a couple of small plantation-cottage-type inns. If we were in Poipu or Princeville, it would be a different story.

I also googled Adam Harjo, the photographer I'd met with the drone. I found quite a few in Oklahoma, and I then narrowed it down to Kaua'i. The Adam Harjo I was looking for had his own website on which he featured his photography. I was surprised that his portfolio didn't comprise only images of newlyweds by waterfalls and on the beach. He had landscapes from both Kaua'i and the Mainland, mostly in New Mexico, where he was originally from. The layered red, orange, and white volcanic rock structures in his home state reminded me of Waimea Canyon. Maybe that's what called him to Kaua'i. He also had a blog, in which he mused about the preservation of indigenous culture and the environment. "If we lose this natural beauty, we won't be able to get it back, no matter how much money we spend," he wrote. I was impressed that he thought so deeply about the world.

I went back to Facebook and went through a few Oklahoma Adam Harjos until I found a page connected to the Adam Harjo I had just met. It hadn't been updated in a while. Among his photos were many of him with a cute brown-eyed woman who wore her long black hair in braids. Of course he had a girlfriend. Why was I even entertaining a crush on him when I knew close to nothing about him?

As I was internet-stalking Adam, the teenagers, one by one, came up to me. "Can I get some water?"

"Sure, go ahead."

"Hmm, it sure would be nice to have an ice." These teens didn't know how to be subtle.

"My sistah is not workin' for free." Sophie put an immediate stop to the hints for shave ice. It warmed my heart to hear her defend my worth. "You gotta at least give a quarter."

Her classmates dug into their backpacks and pockets. One found two dollars, which he threw in the pile of coins. I was moved by that one's generosity and got busy making some shave ice. I told them, though, that they couldn't be picky about the flavors, and I chose the syrups that I had in abundance. The ices were smaller than normal, and instead of the plastic bowls that I usually served in, I found some paper cups in the back. Better for the environment, anyways.

I placed them on a tray and set them out on one of the picnic tables, a wooden spoon in each cup. It soon became a game for each of them to guess the flavor of their ice. Even that slight mystery gave them all such a delight. Funny how something as simple as a shave ice could bring them joy.

Sophie told them to clean up after they were finished, and I gratefully watched as they threw their soggy cups into our metal trash can.

The pandemic was affecting us in all sorts of ways. The isolation was making us slow down and examine ourselves. I noticed that Sophie's usual defiance toward me was weakening. We were on the same boat on these rough waters, so we both figured that it was easier to work together than to fight.

Around lunchtime, we went into our back pantry and pulled out loaves of white bread, peanut butter, and guava jelly. We set it all out on the picnic tables and let them fix their own sandwiches. We were breaking all sorts of social-distancing rules, but at this point it was too hard to do everything by the book.

I was standing in the parking lot, watching the kids finish their lunch, when the Lees' red minivan pulled in front of the flower shop. Nobody had come in yet and I figured business was slow.

Court and her big belly were struggling to get out from the passenger's side, and I ran to help her. Kelly, on the other hand, totally ignored her and went to unlock the shop.

"What's going on?" I asked as Court leaned on my left shoulder. Her eyes were wet and red, and it seemed obvious that they'd been fighting.

Before she could answer, Kelly was back outside with his laptop in his hand. "Leilani, you can take Court home, yah?"

"I can, but—" Before I could receive any clarification, Kelly was back in the driver's seat and speeding away, red rock spitting out in the van's wake.

I lifted my hands up in confusion while Court burst into tears in response.

We went into the quiet flower shop. I opened the back door to let the air go through while Court removed her soggy cloth mask and collapsed in one of the folding chairs around the work table in the middle of the store. I got her a bottle of cold water from the store's refrigerator, and she nodded thanks.

"Kelly's gone," she said.

"Whatchu mean 'gone'?" I felt my face grow cold.

"He went to Hanalei. To work the kalo fields with Pekelo. He's gonna stay at Rick's house during the week and come home on the weekends."

"Oh—" I exhaled in relief. Kelly wasn't gone from the marriage. Just gone from the flower business.

"I told him he didn't have to do that now. Business is bound to pick up, as things are opening up."

"I don't know if they will be opening up much in Waimea, Court. He's just tryin' to make some extra money."

"We've been fine."

"Court." I sat forward in my chair across the table from her. "Have you looked at your accounts recently?"

Court frowned and shook her head. "I've left that up to Mom and Dad." Absorbing the look on my face, she pushed herself up. "Why? What do you know?"

"It's just when I was up at Uncle Rick's, Pekelo was sayin' that maybe things at the flower shop weren't going so good."

"What?" Court waddled toward their old desktop computer. It took a while to boot up.

"I mean, I don't know all the details."

She focused on the computer screen. She clicked, moved the mouse around, and clicked again. "What have my parents done? I told them to apply for a PPP loan. Here it is. Blank."

"Maybe too much for them?"

"I shouldn't have let them take over again! What was I thinkin'?"

"Court, chill out. No get so excited."

"I need to talk to them about this, right now." Court pulled her purse strap from her chair. "Oh, I need a ride."

I went back to Santiago's to pick up a couple of things before getting into the Ford with Court. She was a girl on fire, and I felt a little bad for Court's parents. She was going to let them have it. Court was like lilikoi syrup, sweet as could be, but then came the tang. When she was upset, she could let the best of them have it.

The Lees lived in a neat, brown one-story ranch-style house close to the elementary school. It was sad to see so many empty parking spaces in front of the campus, which was on a hybrid schedule, with students coming in only one or two days a week. I wondered how Dani would remember this time when she got older. She loved to spend time by herself, just drawing, so staying in the bedroom she shared with Sophie wasn't as tortuous as I imagined it was for more active, social kids. But based on the darkness I'd been seeing in her recent illustrations, the uncertainty of our times was seeping into her unconscious.

"Go easy on them," I told Court before she got out of the car. I had a soft spot for the Lees, especially the mister. "This time's been hard on everyone. People not acting quite right."

"But they could have told me. I deserved at least dat much." She closed the door and trudged up the driveway to her parents' side door.

I don't know if I believe in Jesus like Court and at least the old Kelly, but I feel there's some higher power or creator out there. It's hard not to think that, when you live amid such beauty in Kaua'i. Either way, I said a prayer for Court and her marriage. It was still young and tender and I didn't want it to break, especially with a baby on the way.

Before I left, I glanced at my phone and saw a text from Sammie two hours earlier. *Yumi Hara is now conscious!* I was so elated that I wanted to pump my fist in victory. The woman was alive. I could have told Court, but I didn't want to interrupt her showdown.

I could have then gone straight back to Santiago's, to those needy teenagers and the monotony of doing nothing. But Yumi Hara was now out of her coma. So I drove to the hospital and spied Sammie administering a COVID test to someone in a Toyota Corolla. I parked in a side lot and took out a blue-paper medical gown, the one donated by the truck driver, from the back seat. I pulled my hair back in a messy bun and put on a surgical mask and then a plastic visor over that. I looked like any other medical worker in the hospital. Taking a deep breath, I walked into the hospital, trying to look like I belonged.

I'd been in the hospital numerous times, as we Santiagos were always dealing with broken bones and cuts. And there was my mother, of course. She got most of her treatments for her MS from the larger hospital in Līhuʻe, but I'd taken her to this closer one when she took a minor fall a while ago.

There was no one at the reception table. The check-in window was behind glass, and someone with an appointment was talking through her mask to the clerk.

I saw another medical worker wearing a lanyard walking in through a side door and purposefully walked behind her as if I were on staff.

I knew the inside of the hospital well enough to know where the ICU was. On the wall was a huge whiteboard identifying patients and what rooms they were in.

"I thought I saw you come in," said a familiar female voice.

I jumped and turned to see Sammie. "Damn, you scared me. How did you recognize me?"

"Your Crocs. The hospital doesn't allow staff to wear those."

Damn. Foiled again by my fashion choices.

Sammie didn't scold me or rat me out. It was almost like she'd expected me to infiltrate her workplace. "She's not there."

My eyes returned to the whiteboard. "Whatchu mean?" Had Yumi Hara been transferred to a regular room?

"She's gone."

"She just got out of her coma!"

"She's gone, Leilani. She's strong, a lot stronger than she looks. Her vitals were fine. She checked herself out about an hour ago. We couldn't stop her. She took her clothes and left."

"So you don't know where she went?"

"Patients have privacy rights." It was strange to hear Sammie speak so professionally. She'd grown up a lot in the past year.

"Can't Andy do someting?"

She shook her head. "It's not like she did some kind of crime, aside from breaking quarantine earlier. She's tested negative for COVID, so she's good on that front."

Thank God for that.

"What about the rash on her chest?"

"It was an allergic reaction to the mokihana berries. Some people are super-allergic to it. I guess she'd never encountered the berries before. Either way, the Lees shoulda warned her."

I wondered who served Yumi that Sunday morning.

"Oh, by the way, I got some photos from the crime scene from Andy. I couldn't bear to look at them at the time, so I haven't sent them to you."

"You don't have to look. Just email dem to me."

Sammie's phone dinged and she glanced at the screen. "I gotta go back out." She gestured as if I were to go with her.

On the curb she waved me off. "Maybe Yumi Hara will just remain a mystery woman. A mermaid. Came out of the sea and went back."

My heart ached as I thought about never finding out the truth about her. Maybe I was just making too big of a deal of it. She was probably just a money-hungry travel agent from Japan looking for new ways to get her pandemic-weary clients into Kaua'i.

Just worry about yourself, Leilani, I told myself.

When I returned to Waimea Junction, the picnic tables were empty. Sophie and Dani had left the two extension cords out, and a few crumpled paper cups were on the ground. The door to our shave ice shack was unlocked, and I felt my blood boil. Those ungrateful little bakatares, I thought. At least they could clean up after themselves. I knew I should start thinking about making dinner for the crew, but I was sick of them all.

I texted Emily:

Instant ramen for dinner. Everyone cooks for herself.

She sent back a thumbs-up.

I sat in the silent shack, not bothering to turn on the lights. Enough sun was coming through the cracks in the wood that I could see the spiderwebs forming in the high corners.

I was feeling desperate and so alone, lonely enough to start typing his name: T-R-A . . .

I hesitated a moment, and, before my sane side could stop me, I typed: *Hey*

A line of gray dots appeared on my screen, proof that the person on the other side was responding. And then: *Hey. How are you? I was thinking about you.*

When?

Today

You lie

You know me too well. Maybe last week. How are you?

Lousy

At least you're in Hawaii. Raining here.

But I loved the rain. Kaua'i had its share of rain, but more on the North Shore than Waimea.

Travis kept typing: *I miss you.*

There it was. What I wanted. That I was missed. But what would this lead to? I immediately regretted reaching out to Travis.

My throat became dry and my fingers couldn't move. Finally I typed: *Oh, gotta go.*

The flicker of the three dots and then nothing. I couldn't blame him. I had run away from the conversation as soon as he wrote *I miss you.*

To be honest, I didn't know if I actually missed my ex-boyfriend. Mostly I missed someone by my side. I missed all the social activities we did together in Seattle. But him specifically? I wasn't sure.

While I was bent over my phone, I didn't notice that someone was looming in the shack's doorway. It was an outline of a man, his shoulders sloped like an old person's.

I stood up, leaving the phone on the counter. "Sorry, mister, we're closed."

The man moved inside the shack, and I was able to make out his face and clothing. He wore his thinning hair back in a ponytail. An outdated haole fashion statement, but his clothing was more establishment: a Tommy Bahama shirt sporting splashes of hibiscus, a shirt that would have set him back a hundred dollars. I knew the brand well because Dad had the company's catalogues all over the house. As Tommy

Santiago, former hotshot professional surfer, he was trying to capture the Tommy Bahama market with a more urban flair—but, based on sales, he was floundering.

"Uh, no shave ice today." Maybe he didn't speak English?

"Looks like your business has taken a hit."

"Ah, who are you?"

I flipped the switch to the lights and recognized the long face and prominent nose from those photos on the website for Garvin Washburne, JD. The long hair was a new development, but during the pandemic we'd all adopted ridiculous hairstyles.

"I'm Garvin Washburne. I believe you were at my house on Alealea Road."

My mouth fell open. What the hell was he doing at Santiago's?

"Since you paid me a visit, I thought I'd pay your business a visit. Why were you at my personal residence so early in the morning?"

"Ah. . . ." I wasn't sure if I should mention Yumi Hara. I couldn't come up with anything that made sense. "I don't know if I should talk with you. With everything that happened, you know."

"What happened, from your perspective?" In spite of his silly ponytail, Garvin commanded respect. His voice sounded like it could be on public radio.

Words spilled out of my mouth. "I was making a flower delivery. I help my friend out with her business. Right next door. Lee's Leis and Flowers."

"I never received any flowers."

"Well. . . ." There was nothing more I could say.

"I'm ready to get them now."

"Huh?"

"You said I was supposed to receive some flowers." Chills went up my spine. His manner of speaking was so monotone, expressionless, which freaked me out more than anything. This was the man who'd shot Arkansas Ted down. Why had Ted been so set on hacking Washburne with Pekelo's machete?

"That arrangement is pah, no good. From yesterday. Had to throw it out."

"I can wait for a new one." He stared at me with his eagle eyes, daring me to break down and say the truth. Which made me all the more determined to stay on course.

"Okay." I had an extra key to Lee's.

As soon as I opened the flower shop, I prayed that there'd be some blooms in the refrigerator worth salvaging. I exhaled upon seeing some. A lobster claw whose red brilliance had started to yellow. Two stalks of birds of paradise, one day from their crowns withering. At least they had plenty of long, healthy leaves of the ti plant, green smeared with purplish-red streaks. We'd go tropical today.

I filled a tall vase with water and started with the framing of the ti leaves before pushing in the lobster claw and then the birds of paradise into the center.

Washburne, who had followed me into the flower shop, examined my creation. Not perfect, but good enough.

"Was there a card with this?"

"Ah, yeah." I pretended to look through some paper records and wrote on a card, *Thanks. The boys of Zeta Alpha Pi.* I handed him that and a packet of cut-flower preservative.

Washburne stared at the card for a long time, more time than the brief message required to absorb.

"You're good," he finally said.

"Well, I try my best."

"Cut the bullshit," he said. "I don't know what you're after, but I'll find out."

I was genuinely shocked, but feigned that I had no idea what he was talking about. "Excuse me, mister? Are you unhappy with the arrangement?"

"You weren't at my home to deliver flowers. That much I know. You've been all around the island with that scooter of yours, asking questions. You don't want to overstep, Miss Santiago. I'm familiar with your family members. You wouldn't want anything to happen to them."

My mama-bear anger pulsed up my body. "Are you threatening my family?"

"Just keep quiet and I'll have no problems with you." With that, he and his ponytail left the shop.

"Ah, you forgot your flowers," I murmured. But we both knew he didn't care about them. I watched him drive off in a maroon Lexus with the license plate WASHATTY1. More like SHITATTY.

I tried to process what Washburne had said. Why was I such a threat to him? And who did he know in my family? I figured it had to be my father, considering all the legal problems he'd been involved in. But the scooter? Why did he know that I sometimes rode the scooter, most recently to Lydgate? He hadn't been the one on that motorcycle, but perhaps he had hired someone to follow me.

Seeking help, I took my flower arrangement over to D-man's. His corner of Waimea Junction was already lively, and it wasn't even past seven.

A couple of the regulars, beers in their hands, nodded toward me. Only the tourists usually ordered multicolored drinks with paper umbrellas and fresh fruits.

"Hey, Leilani, long time no see."

I placed the arrangement on the counter.

"What's this?"

"Thought it could brighten up the place."

"Mahalo." D-man accepted my gift, but I could tell from the look he gave me that he knew something was up.

Taking a seat on one of the high stools, I commented "You've been busy."

"A pandemic leads people to drink."

And smoke. I felt like a cigarette right now, but I squelched the urge.

"Hey, I've come up with a new Japanese mixed sake drink. You wanna try?"

"Sure." I mostly drank sake warm in sushi bars. I liked the kick that sake had, how it warmed the throat and belly. I could use some warming up now.

D-man handed me a light-colored drink in a cold martini glass. This was sake?

I took a cautious sip. Smooth and tangy. "Mmmm, that's good. Fresh lemon juice, right?"

"With some simple syrup."

"What do you call it?"

"Yoko's Lemon Drop."

"Who's Yoko?"

"You don't need to know, Leilani." Actually, I was happy to hear that there was a new woman in D-man's life. He and my mother had a longtime connection, and I was frankly worried that their close friendship might merge into something more.

"Where's your old man?"

"O'ahu. Trying to make a deal with ABC for making Killer Wave masks."

"Oh, yah. He betta change the name of dat company. No one wants to hear about Killer Waves right now."

Good point. Only I wasn't going to be the person to break that to my father.

A couple of regulars joined me at the surfboard counter. D-man was getting their beers when my phone dinged with a text. I was surprised to see that it was from the latest addition to my phone book.

It's Adam.

Yeah, I know.

Hey, you interested in maybe getting a bite to eat sometime?

I paused for moment. Really, this was happening? I was being asked on a date during the pandemic?

Sure. After dinner would be better. I have to cook for my family. I'll be in Waimea tomorrow.

K. Text me & we can figure it out.

After my text exchange with Adam, I returned to my Yoko's Lemon Drop. Yoko's had a wallop of alcohol—I felt my line of vision move up and down, like I was on a boat. I was a lightweight when it came to drinking, a trait that I definitely hadn't inherited from my father.

After serving some other customers, D-man returned to me. "What's up, Leilani? And don't tell me you came over to give me flowers."

I tried the best I could to explain what had happened the morning before and then Washburne's surprise visit. I left out the threat, because I didn't need D-man to overreact right now.

"Have you heard about this lawyer?" I asked, as casually as possible.

"What's his name again?"

"Garvin Washburne."

D-man looked past his surfboard counter in thought. "No, nevah heard of him. But I think he and I run in different circles."

"He doesn't want me to poke in his business."

"Well, lawyers. I'm sure he has some dirt he's trying to hide."

Washburne's long face loomed in front of me, morphing into something more sinister. "He's lying about Ted," I declared, more to myself than D-man. In my tipsiness, that much was clear to me. He had not shot Ted in self-defense. But the question was why.

"Give me another," I told D-man. I didn't know the answer to my question; but for a night, I wanted a break from thinking about it at all.

Saturday

Chapter Eleven

I'M NOT QUITE SURE how I got home last night, but when I woke I was still in the clothes that I had worn the day before. I was in a tangle of sheets, and I'd rolled off my foam mattress. This was ridiculous. I would need to borrow a sleeping bag from Court or someone else in my circle. Emily was not in her bed. I patted my pockets and then pulled at my sheets in an effort to find my phone. It was nowhere to be found, so I pulled myself up and opened the bedroom door.

The blast of light blinded me, shooting pain in the front of my head. It felt like someone was doing acupuncture to my brain. Before I could fully regain my senses, Sophie handed me my phone. "You ready to go?"

I covered my eyes. "Go where?"

"You promised you gonna take me out driving. Today. Saturday."

I needed coffee. I stumbled to the kitchen and was frustrated to see that none had been made. The Santiago women were useless.

Sophie followed me into the kitchen like she was a hungry dog. I was starting to remember that I'd made some promise to her about driving. Damn me. "Let me just get some coffee in me, okay?"

Even the grinding of my coffee beans was insufferable. This morning wasn't a Mr. Coffee type of day. I took out my

French press and emptied the grinder into the glass carafe. When the water in the kettle was close to boiling, I carefully poured it over the grinds, pushed down on the top, and waited for my magic brew to be completed. Sophie knew me well enough to remain quiet until I poured my first cup. I usually drank my coffee black, but today I fortified it with a couple of teaspoons of sugar and some dried milk.

"You were drunk last night," Sophie finally declared, eyeing me from across the kitchen table.

I was afraid to hear what I had done, but I had to ask. "What happened?"

"D-man drove you home in the Ford. You were babbling a lot about that lawyer, Washburne. And also that lady we found in Waimea Bay."

Oh my God. I couldn't believe I'd voiced my obsessions out loud. Then I remembered my text exchange with Adam Harjo. Did I imagine that?

"Who heard me?"

"Basically everyone in the house. Mom even came out of her room and sat on the porch with D-man for a while. I think she's pretty sad."

"She is? About me?"

"No, not about you." I had never spoken to Mom about her sadness, but I knew that with her MS, she didn't want to squander any active years that she had left. She had discussed taking the whole brood to her hometown in Orange County. Dani had been talking nonstop about going to Disneyland. But that was all in the *before* times.

"I know she was happy that you said you were going to teach me how to drive."

I gave her a side eye. She was a master manipulator.

"Where's Em?"

"She went to Santiago's to study. She said she wants the car this afternoon, so we have to be back by two."

The gigantic clock by the refrigerator said it was eleven. "Well, let's get going then."

My father was the one who had taught me to drive. Actually, I was behind the wheel from probably age fourteen. Dad knew the least populated places on the island, and when it was just the two of us he'd grin and say, "You wanna drive?"

We'd bounce over dirt roads amid kalo fields. One time I almost lost control and came close to crashing into a palm tree. I screeched to a halt and looked nervously at Dad in the driver's seat. His teeth were brilliant white against his dark skin as he let out screeches of laughter. "Numba one rule: Don't let trees smash you."

He took the wheel back after that almost-accident. But days later we went out again and again. Dad always seemed to give us girls multiple chances to redeem ourselves. In that sense, he was more generous with us than with himself.

I tried to keep that in mind as I sat in the passenger seat. I had forgotten how tall Sophie had gotten these past couple of years. She was only a couple of inches from my height and didn't have to adjust the driver's seat much to be able to reach the brake and gas pedals.

I told her to drive toward Kaua'i Community College. Since students were mostly taking their classes online, the parking lot was wide open, perfect for practicing turns and parallel parking. It was about a thirty-minute drive on the highway, which was again relatively empty. And anyway, Kaua'i's main highway was like a regular boulevard in a city. I rolled down the window and let the late-morning ocean air blow on my face, still a bit puffy from all the alcohol I'd consumed last night.

Once we arrived in the parking lot, she looked at me for instruction. "Let's see how you are at backing into a parking spot." I pointed to a designated space.

She first steered wide and then corrected herself. I had her do this a couple of times before working on parallel parking. I got out of the car and dragged some dried palm fronds to simulate parked cars. "Park right in the middle of them."

This effort was a little more tricky. If the fronds had actually been cars, Sophie would have knocked off a couple of bumpers. She just needed to practice. I vowed that I'd go out with her more regularly. Her getting her driver's license when she turned sixteen would certainly lessen the household load on me, especially when Kaua'i opened up.

"So, what do you want to be?" I finally said on our way home.

"Whatchu mean?"

"You know, for a job."

"I want to go to Tokyo. And produce some anime or video games."

"I don't think you can go straight from high school. You probably need to go to college. Or go to the Mainland and get some experience in a company. Talk to Sean. He knows about these things."

"You do too."

"I know notting about anime or video games."

"You went to UW. Everyone says that's a big deal."

"But I didn't finish. Em can tell you a lot more about what moves you should make."

"I don't want to be a lawyer."

It warmed my heart to hear that Sophie didn't idolize Emily as much as I thought she did.

"How come you came back home?" she asked me point-blank.

I'd never had this level of conversation with Sophie. She was fifteen going on sixteen now, heading toward adulthood. It felt strange to talk to her like a peer. It was uncomfortable, but also freeing, like our past irritations and identities were flying out the car window.

"Mom was a big reason," I had to admit. I would never state it so clearly to our mother, because I wouldn't want her to feel guilty. "Also, I realize now that I'd lost my footing on the Mainland. I had to come back to be more integrated." *Integrated* was a word I would never use in family conversations, but it perfectly represented who I was now.

"Santiago's was becoming a success because of you."

I was shocked to hear this pronouncement from, of all people, Sophie. I let her words bathe me in warmth.

"Really. You were the only person who could persuade Baachan to stop using that old cash register. And you made Santiago's more fancy. My friends were taking selfies at Santiago's. Nobody did that before."

"Well, that's old news." I brushed aside Sophie's compliments. I didn't want to dissolve into tears.

"You have good ideas, Leilani. You can come up with some new ones."

We were together for about two hours. Sophie was actually a pretty good driver, calm behind the wheel. When a pickup truck almost cut her off, she didn't lose her cool. Me, I was probably more like our father, temperamental and reactionary. And out for revenge. Road rage didn't fit the culture in Hawai'i, especially on a small island like Kaua'i.

The only time you heard drivers honk their horns was to get roosters out of the middle of the road. Anytime else was considered the ultimate expression of rudeness.

Since we had this opportunity away from the house, I felt that I had to dig a little deeper about Ro. "Mrs. Ramos's boyfriend, Roger. You know much about him?"

"Only that he's dog shit." I let Sophie's foul mouth go unchecked. Who was I to tell my sister how to talk?

"He do anyting to Ro?" My heart pounded hard. I braced myself for what I would hear.

"Nah, not at least anyting that Ro would say. But if he had the chance. . . ."

I gritted my teeth. I got the message.

When we arrived home, Emily was sitting by herself at the dining room table, staring at her phone screen.

"Hey," I said, removing my Crocs by the front door while Sophie ran out back to talk to Ro. "We back. You can take the car."

No response. Her arm was frozen in place as if the phone had become permanently attached to her fingers.

"Ah, Em—"

"Won't need the car. Going to stay in." Em's voice was robotic. Had something happened between the two lovebirds?

I slid into a chair on the other side of the table. "What's wrong?"

"I got some bad news."

"What?" My mind immediately went to Dad. Had something happened to him in O'ahu?

"My scholarship might be pulled. I think I have to drop out of law school."

"But why? Because of the pandemic?"

"They didn't say."

Emily remained in a trance-like state, and I pulled the phone from her grip.

It was an email sent to her Gmail account.

Dear Emily Santiago:
We regret to inform you that because of our 2021 budgetary issues,
we may not be able to continue your scholarship into the next
semester. We will keep you informed of any new developments.

It was signed by the executive director of the Filipino and Pacific Islander Future Lawyers Fund.

"This is bullshit," I said. "How can they grant you a year-long scholarship and then take it back?"

"It's the pandemic. Things happen."

"Rich people are just getting richer right now." The sales rep at the Big Island–based coffeehouse had gotten me interested in following the stock market. From my work at the Seattle high-tech company, I had a small amount of money in a 401(k), and I noticed that after the pandemic broke out in the US, my retirement investment had taken an immediate small dip but now was steadily rising. "Keep studying. You are not dropping out."

I placed the phone screen-down on the table. I cursed the executive director of the fund and went to the bedroom to retrieve my laptop. Sitting on the floor with my back against the twin-bed frame, I googled the future lawyers fund. The nonprofit had a simple website with a list of past recipients and an application for 2021. There was no message that the fund was struggling. I clicked on a button that explained the origins of the organization. It had been started in the 1980s in Hawai'i and was designed to help specifically Filipino Americans and Pacific Islanders who were underrepresented in law schools around the nation. The executive director was a Filipino man—young and pleasant-looking. Born in Oʻahu, he had attended UCLA and gained his law degree from UW (yay, Huskies!). He didn't fit the evil profile I had imagined. Maybe the fund was losing money from donors?

I went down to view the members of the board of directors. There were local television anchors, professors of Native Hawaiian Studies, and then, at the very end, the cleaned-up corporate version of Garvin Washburne wearing a gray suit and blue tie instead of a polo shirt with hibiscus flowers.

The asshole. I knew this was no coincidence. In my limited experience with the criminal justice system, effective lawyers were sharks, able to smell blood and weakness in even the darkest waters. The shark Garvin Washburne had somehow figured out my Achilles' heel—my family—and had deftly come out of nowhere to snatch away our collective dream, a future for Emily.

I'd keep your mouth shut, he had warned me. What was he so afraid of? What had Ted had on him?

I tried to find more information on Washburne on the internet. He was originally from Rhode Island but received his undergraduate degree from UCLA and his law degree from the University of Arizona. He started his private practice in Phoenix before moving to Honolulu. He seemed involved primarily in real estate law but also seemed to have his hand in a bit of everything—estate planning, family law, and even slip-and-fall.

I'd heard enough about law firms from Emily to know that this kind of general practice was unusual. Everyone specialized, and the law was different for every niche. Maybe in Hawai'i there was only room for generalists who did a bit of everything.

I found one feature story on Washburne in the University of Arizona alumni magazine. It explained that his work in forging retirement-home development deals had brought him to Hawai'i. Once he stepped foot in the Islands, he was hooked. He'd been working for forty years, and it seemed like he wanted a quieter life on a smaller island. My guess was that Washburne was pushing for a return to tourism faster than anyone else was ready for. Maybe that was the connection with Arkansas? Was there a steady stream of tourists to Hawai'i from that state? I googled Hawai'i and Arkansas and discovered an article about an exchange between the two states to create "bubble" campuses at respective hotels. Petitions opposing the program had been circulated in Hawai'i, one titled "Stop Bringing Nonresident Students to Hawai'i During a Pandemic," garnering more than 12,000 signatures. As with the frat boys, we didn't want outsiders coming to the Islands at this time.

In the middle of my internet search, a little digital bubble informed me that I'd received an email from Samantha Nunes. The crime-scene photos. I was expecting them to be gory, but Andy hadn't included any shots of the body, which apparently had already been removed. There were yellow plastic markers with the numbers 2, 5, and 7 placed all around the blood-stained tile floor. There was one thing I recognized: the black Arkansas Razorbacks mask that Ted had been wearing the night of the protest.

I was leaning toward my computer screen to get a closer look when I heard a shriek and then some yelling. I rushed out into the hallway. The commotion was happening outside.

"Eh, you not allowed in here!" It was Sophie's voice, uncharacteristically high-pitched. *What now?*

The sounds were coming from the backyard, so I ran through the kitchen to the back screen door.

A man wearing a sleeveless black T-shirt faced the blue mushroom tent. From the look of his oily black hair, I assumed it was Ro's mother's boyfriend, Roger.

My hunch was confirmed when I neared the tent.

Emily and Sophie blocked Roger from the tent, while Dani and Mom stood on the sides and Baachan brandished a broom in the back. The only male on our side was Jimin, who was bobbing his head as he crossed the dirt ground, oblivious to what was happening.

"You come afta Ro, you have to go through us." Sophie dangled her tongue out like a Maori warrior. A fighting spirit inhabited her skinny body. Baachan swept the air with her broom as if she was one of the samurai on her Japanese programs.

"What the hell is going on?" I didn't see Ro, but assumed she was inside the tent.

"Ro needs to come home," Roger insisted. He now wore a full beard. It was unbelievable how fast this man's hair grew. Was he part werewolf?

"You're not her family."

"Marian needs her."

"Where is Mrs. Ramos, anyhow?" I asked.

"She's sick."

"The virus?" I asked.

"No, not that." He wouldn't elaborate further.

"If Mrs. Ramos wants her, she needs to come herself," Emily said in her best threatening lawyer voice.

"She sent me here for her. She needs Ro."

We heard the sound of a zipper loosening, and then Ro appeared, her long hair in disarray from being in the sleeping bag. She pulled out her giant backpack. She was ready to go with Roger.

"Ro, no, don't go." Sophie sounded desperate.

"I have to go. My madda called for me." Ro, with her heavy bag on her back, looked like a wizened wilderness explorer. She had gone to places unknown to Sophie.

"Leilani!" Sophie was pleading me to intervene.

"You don't understand, Sophie." Ro, who was about Sophie's height, looked her BFF in the eye. "You got your sistahs. My madda only has me."

Ro's declaration silenced Sophie, who obviously had never thought about life without all of us.

"Wait. I'll drive you home," I said.

"She goes with me," Roger attempted to pull Ro closer to him, causing her to resist him with a sharp elbow.

"No, she goes with me." *Who are you?* I thought. *You have no rights to Ro.*

Sophie was completely undone. She let out a shriek of expletives, and I didn't blame her. Dani turned her head away, her crown of blond hair shielding her temporarily from her older sister's pain.

I ran into the kitchen and threw some loose granola bars and a mango in a plastic bag before taking Ro with me in the Ford.

Ro was quiet during our drive east on the highway. Anger and despair pulsed throughout my body. What if the home was unsafe? Would I have the nerve to call DCFS?

As soon as I stopped the car in front of her house, Ro ran out, lugging her backpack with both hands. She disappeared through the security gate before I could give her my sack of snacks. We'd arrived before Roger, and just then his pickup truck, blasting Jethro Tull through the open windows, pulled into the gravel driveway. Roger ran to beat me to the front door.

"Bitch, you can go now," he said, locking the security gate behind him.

"Mrs. Ramos, are you okay? Ro?" I called out through the metal grate.

I thought I spied Mrs. Ramos on the couch, wrapped in blankets, with Ro kneeling by her side. Then the door slammed shut.

I looped the handles of the plastic bag of snacks around the knob of the security gate. Who was I fooling? Granola bars and mangoes weren't going to make a dent in this problem.

I got in the car and sat outside the chain-link fence for a few minutes. I searched on my phone and found the agency I was looking for. I hesitated for a moment. I felt that I had no choice. I put my finger on the Department of Children and Family Services link and called.

When I arrived home, everyone was siloed into their own spaces except for Baachan, who sat at the dining room table. She looked like her spine had been yanked out of her body. She was uncharacteristically silent.

"You okay?"

"Hammajang." She didn't have to say anything more. Everything was messed up. I had been miserable about what the pandemic had taken from me, but realized now that I had more than other folks like Ro had.

I couldn't bear to tell Baachan what I had done. The word would get to Sophie, and I couldn't deal with drama tonight.

Baachan sucked her loose cheeks as if she was trying to extract something lost deep in her gray matter. "Sōka!" she finally announced. "Dat Washburne, I know where I seen him before. At Rocket Nakayama's court thingy."

"Whatchu mean, court thingy? You mean hearing?"

"He in trouble for buying some drugs. Washburne his lawyer."

My phone dinged with a text.

I'm in your neighborhood. You available?

Damn. I had forgotten about Adam.

Sorry, I texted back. *Kinda crazy right now. Can we talk tonight?*

I wasn't sure if Adam was a phone person. It was hard these days to figure out a new friend's communication language—text, phone, Snapchat, email. . . .

Facetime? he wrote.

I guess he's a Facetime man, which didn't surprise me, because as a photographer he was visually oriented. I personally didn't care for it much because it meant I'd have to make sure nothing was stuck in my teeth. But I was standing him up for drinks, so I would make that compromise.

I sent him the thumbs-up emoticon. We decided to touch base at eight.

Okay, focus, Leilani, I told myself. I remembered what Baachan told me, but before I could follow up she had retreated to her bedroom. It was just as well, as it was close to dinnertime. Leilani-rella—yeah, that was me—had to return to the kitchen. We had run out of chicken, even frozen ones. I made a big pot of gohan, this time taking care about how much water I added to the rice. On the inside refrigerator door compartment, I found a jar of umeboshi—fat red pickled plums—and a container of seaweed paste that Baachan had gotten from a friend. We still had some cans of tuna; I opened two, dumped the contents into a bowl, and added generous spoons of mayonnaise and black pepper. When the rice cooker sounded that it was ready, Baachan drifted into the kitchen, followed by Dani. They glanced at the condiments I'd assembled and figured out what I was up to.

Dani began cutting sheets of dried nori in half while Baachan washed her hands vigorously with soap. I unplugged the rice cooker and moved it to the kitchen table. Dani pressed the button for the lid to pop open, and the steam moistened her eyelashes and the front of her hair. We sat quietly as we took turns placing mounds of hot rice in our bare hands, squeezing it gently, and forming a hole for a red plum, black seaweed paste, or tuna mayo. Once each was filled, we formed triangles while Dani dressed each with a half sheet of nori and lined them up neatly on a platter. She made individual plates of musubi for Mom and Sophie. Mom was regularly eating in her and Dad's bedroom for safety's sake, and tonight Sophie had withdrawn into her cocoon of anime books to blunt the pain of Ro's removal.

About 7:30, I left the kitchen to take a shower and brush my teeth. I blew my hair dry and even put on tinted moisturizer and mascara, something I hadn't done since the start of the pandemic. I went outside on the back porch, where the mushroom tent was still visible on the dirt ground. I turned on our electric lantern and adjusted my hair in my phone camera. My face looked fuzzy in the darkness, which was just fine with me.

Adam called promptly at eight. I was glad, because I
don't like to wait for anyone. He was inside a well-lit structure made of light wooden beams. He said he was sorry to
hear that things had been so chaotic for me.

"Yeah, well." I didn't want to get into all the details right
now. "Where do you live, anyway?"

"I'm in Līhu'e."

"Līhu'e? I thought you were living on the North
Shore."

"I was. I've been going up there every day to finish up
a video program. But I have my own place now on Hana-
maulu Rim."

"Are you there now?"

"Yup. You want a tour?" With jerky Facetime views, he
showed me a very bare two-bedroom house. Some of the
flooring looked unfinished. There was a sleeping bag on the
floor of one of the bedrooms.

"Hey, that looks familiar," I said.

"You too? I was living at my friend's place in Hanalei.
That was all furnished. So I'm starting from scratch."

"Nice," I said. What a feeling it would be to start fresh
without any physical baggage from the past.

"Yeah, the previous owners from the Mainland didn't
have enough money for the remodel. And then I got an
inheritance from my grandmother, who died last year." He
seemed a bit embarrassed about his windfall.

"Impressive to buy someting in Hawai'i during a
pandemic."

"It almost doesn't seem right."

"You different than the oddah folks coming from the
Mainland and buying up land. You making a life here. Your
grandmother would have wanted it." I surprised myself by

saying such platitudes. It felt good to be connecting with someone who was experiencing some good fortune.

"This is why I was out your way." He aimed his phone toward a toilet that was sitting in the middle of what looked like a bathroom.

"You got a toilet in Waimea? Who from?"

"Some folks who live near the Buddhist temple. Names are the Sakanashis."

"Oh, I know them. They my baachan's friends."

"They say they never used this one."

"Oh, yeah." I had no reason to dispute that information but wondered why the Sakanashis had a spare toilet lying around. "So you have no working toilet right now."

"I have two bathrooms. One working and the other one unfinished."

"You have two bathrooms in a two-bedroom house? Ahrite! You rich!"

We both laughed. It felt so good to talk about something so mundane (but necessary) like toilets. I realized that I hadn't really laughed since before the pandemic.

"You're a good writer, by the way," I said as I slapped away a mosquito from my calf. Laughing seemed to increase my boldness.

Adam's eyes grew wide and he pulled at his man bun. I wondered how long his hair was, down. He was obviously moved by my compliment.

"I read your blog," I explained.

"Oh, I haven't updated it in a while."

"Why did you leave New Mexico?"

"It was for a girl."

"It's always for a girl," I said. "Except in my case. I left a boy in Seattle for Hawai'i."

"Sorry."

"Nah, it was for the betta." The minute I said that, I knew I meant it.

"Me too. It didn't work out. Then I fell in love with Kaua'i."

"You don't feel island fever?" I could imagine if you were raised in the American Southwest, the stretches of land would feel endless. Here, you could only drive so far before you hit the edge of a cliff overlooking the sea.

"Nah. Maybe that's where the drone helps me see Kaua'i differently. Not from the land. But the air."

"Those drones can get kinda annoying." I had to be honest.

"Fo' sure. Don't like the tourists sneaking them into parks and things. In my culture, it's all about respect."

Adam explained that he was from the Navajo nation. I had met Native Americans before in Seattle, only they were from Los Angeles or from reservations that fished in area rivers and lakes.

"Don't you feel lonely being away from your family?"

"They're spread all over the US now. There's really not one place that I can call home. That's why I feel connected to Kaua'i. The 'aina, right? And everyone is happy to come here and visit me."

"It's been hard for me, coming back here to live." In the darkness in front of the mushroom tent, I exposed myself more than I'd expected to. "Especially in the pandemic."

"Yeah, I get it. If I didn't have this drone project, I'd be in hot water."

"No, I'm not talking only about the business." I shared with Adam about my encounter with Yumi Hara. "So that day I saw you, I kind of lied to you, or at least let you believe a lie. I wasn't there to deliver flowers to anyone in Hanalei. I was there to spy on Yumi's Airbnb." I moved my phone so the camera lens wouldn't show my face. What a thing to confess before we even went out.

"Sheeeeet." And then chuckling. I returned the phone to my face and was surprised to see Adam smiling. "I knew you were lying. You're not good at it, Leilani. I just figured it was for a good reason."

I felt warmth fill my lower body. So Adam wasn't judging me. He barely knew me, and yet he was giving me the benefit of the doubt.

Jimin suddenly let out the most blood-curdling sound. Why in the world would a rooster be crowing at nine o'clock at night? He didn't do it just once, but twice and then three times. I had to apologize to Adam, and we made arrangements to touch base later the following week. For me, it wasn't soon enough.

Sunday

Chapter Twelve

I DIDN'T RECOGNIZE the number that rang my cell phone the next day. It was an 808 number, so it probably originated from Hawai'i, although, with all the scam callers who can fake their location, you never know.

"Hello." I made my voice gruff.

"Leilani?"

"Dad. How come you not using your cell phone?"

"I'm using a friend's. Mine lost its charge."

I knew Dad was staying with a friend in O'ahu from his competitive surfing days. Based on the sound of crashing waves, they were at the beach now.

"I think we may be close to making a deal." Dad was trying to contain his excitement, but his voice was about half an octave higher than usual.

Finally. Good news. We needed some now.

"I need you to go to Killer Wave and get some more fabric samples. The newest ones that have come in."

My mind raced to recall the latest delivery. Between running our household, worrying about Ro's and Court's travails, and the distractions of Yumi, Ted's murder, and the lawyer threatening my family, it was difficult to stay on top of anything else.

"Can you send it out today?"

"It's Sunday, Dad. Gonna be kinda hard."

I heard a catch in his throat. For Mr. Toxic Masculinity to show any emotion meant this deal was especially important. "I'll find a way," I told him.

Normally, since it was Sunday, I would have asked Sophie to help, but she hadn't come out of her room ever since Ro left. I hoped she'd never find out that I was the one who'd reported Mrs. Ramos to DCFS. In the meantime, I'd have to complete this mundane task on my own.

Normally I'd be dragging my feet. But talking to Adam had given me feelings that I hadn't had since the early days with Travis. And I'd be seeing him sometime this coming week. So in spite of all the upheaval in my life, there was some sweetness too.

I didn't even bother to fuel myself with coffee. I drove the Fiesta to Waimea Junction. I walked to the rear of Killer Wave to unlock the back storage room and saw the white door of the Porta-Potty open and close. Great. Sean had moved that in for construction workers who were supposed to be repairing our roof before the rainy season. The door was supposed to be locked, but someone had knocked off the flimsy latch weeks ago. Local surfers and food-bank folks were now regular users of the Porta-Potty, making my life as Waimea Junction's unofficial janitor even more miserable. I was ready to give the trespasser a piece of my mind when I came face-to-face with a woman in an oversized T-shirt from the hospital's 5K fundraiser from 2019. "Yumi Hara!" I exclaimed. "What are you doing here?"

"Why you know my name?" She spoke haltingly, spitting out one word at a time.

I really wished I'd been a better student in my high school Japanese class. All I could reasonably manage was counting up to ten and random words like *neko* (cat) and *ie* (house).

It looked like she'd pulled a tarp off of the shack and slept on top of it last night. She was too old to be camping out like this.

"You must be hungry." I put my hand to my mouth to simulate eating.

Yumi nodded.

I let her into Santiago's and raided the pantry for something more nutritious than Kettle chips and Oreos. The best I could come up with was peanut butter cheese crackers.

Yumi had begun to carefully tear off the plastic wrapping when Baachan and Sophie came sauntering inside. Baachan abruptly stopped, almost causing Sophie to crash into her.

"Who dis?" Baachan asked.

Sophie's eyes widened. "It's the mermaid lady. The one we pulled out of the ocean."

Baachan's milky gray eyes absorbed Yumi's figure from head to toe. The oversized T-shirt wasn't making a good impression. "More like pilau tuna fish."

I ignored Baachan's comment. Yumi didn't smell that bad. I was more relieved to see that my grandmother had gotten my sister out of the house. "Oh, good. I need you to translate for me," I said.

"I told you to use Google Translate," Sophie reminded me.

"Well, you two are here now." I should have insisted that Sophie and Baachan wear masks, but that would make it harder to communicate. I sat them down on the other side of the table and opened both doors for the breeze to blow through the shack, causing a few napkins on the counter to flutter to the ground.

"Now what?" Sophie asked.

"*Nihongo*," I pointed to Sophie and Baachan, indicating to Yumi that both of them spoke Japanese. Then to my amateur family translators: "Ask her why she spent the night here." If she had access to a credit card, she could have easily returned to her posh rental in Hanalei.

Yumi took a deep breath. "*Musume o sagashiteru.*"

My sister and grandmother exchanged looks.

"*Musume*, dat's daughta, yah?" Baachan said.

"She's looking for her daughter," Sophie said definitely.

A runaway, I wondered?

Yumi then released a long line of Japanese words.

"Whoa! Too fast," Baachan exclaimed. She angled one of her giant earlobes toward Yumi's mouth.

The three of them went back and forth. I maybe understood every tenth word, which probably hindered, not helped, my comprehension.

I hated being in the dark. "What about her daughter?" I asked after Yumi finished talking.

Both Sophie's and Baachan's mouths hung open.

Sophie's was the first to close. She swallowed before speaking. "She's saying Courtney is her daughter."

I paced the floor of the shack, trying to figure out what to do.

How could this strange woman from Japan be Court's bio mom? Could she have left her newborn at the Kaua'i fire station? Or was that a made-up story?

Court was ready to pop any moment now. This wasn't the time for her to face such a curveball. Already she'd had to forego the big baby shower she'd always dreamed of because of COVID. She tried to put on a happy face—"I can tell my baby that we had a drive-by shower!" Mrs. Lee, Mom, and I made cute favor bags decorated with baby footprints that Court passed out with cupcakes to friends who drove into Waimea Junction. Baachan tried to add some humor by tying a pillow around her belly underneath her muʻumuʻu—but the truth was, no one except me even noticed. Sophie took photos on her phone, but I knew that, in the end, Court wouldn't treasure these images of her self fully masked, with friends extending their heads out of car windows.

Maybe Yumi was lying? I glanced at her, looking like a kid herself in that huge T-shirt. No, I didn't think so. But maybe she was mistaken? That could be it, right? But she'd traveled all this way to uncover the truth. And how was Garvin Washburne mixed in with all of this? Before I could prepare my follow-up questions, I heard a car door slam outside.

Footsteps, and then—"Hel-lo!" Court, her hand on her hip, pushed her swollen body into the doorway of Santiago's. Seeing that a small crowd had gathered inside, she pulled up her Killer Wave mask. "What's up?" she asked, registering each person around the table.

"Ah—" My throat felt bone-dry.

Court blinked and then focused on Yumi on the other side of the table. "You, the wahine with the mokihana lei. You know how much trouble you cause?"

Yumi was frozen, a strange expression transforming her face. Looking at both of them in the same room made me see the resemblance. Their delicate, almost birdlike builds, their wide jaw lines. There was no doubt in my mind now—they were mother and daughter.

Yumi's eyes had filled with tears, and they dribbled down her cheeks. She didn't attempt to wipe them away. It was as if she welcomed them. "*Utsukushii*," she finally said.

Court frowned. "What?"

"What she wen say?" I asked Sophie, who sat stunned and speechless in her seat.

"Beautiful," she said.

Court was not satisfied with the answer. "What dat got to do with anyting?"

Everyone stared at me. I knew it was my job as the BFF. "Court, she says she's your madda. Your biological one."

"You lolo."

I stayed silent. Sophie looked down at the table, while Baachan pretended that she was transfixed by something in the window.

"I don't understand."

"She came all the way from Japan to find you."

"I was born here on Kaua'i. Left at the firehouse."

"Maybe she can explain," I said.

Court turned the other way. "I have to talk to my parents."

"Of course. I'll drive you. But you have to talk to her, eh? She came all this way."

"I'm not going to be alone with her. And I can't speak Japanese."

"Baachan can help interpret. And I'll be with you."

Baachan whipped her head around, causing her grandma bun to fall into more disarray. She scrunched down and vigorously shook her head. She wanted no part of this family drama.

"And me too," Sophie interjected. "I can help. My Japanese is better than Baachan's."

"Yah, she more betta," Baachan said. Baachan never said anyone else was better than her in anything.

"No, dis not for kids." Sophie was growing up fast, but I feared that this conversation would take her to places she wasn't quite ready for.

"Fine," Sophie declared, getting to her feet. "I'm supposed to meet Ro outside anyway."

The four of us sat in the flower shop, one on each side of the work table. It had more light and space than the shave ice shack.

"I'm here under protest," Baachan declared. Nobody responded. The tension was as thick as day-old mochi in that room. My grandmother's discomfort was the last thing anyone cared about.

Court sat across from Yumi, and both of them stared at each other.

"If you're the mom, who's the dad?" Court said, expecting Baachan to translate. Yumi, however, knew enough English to struggle with an answer on her own.

"I, I—" she hesitated and then poured out a monologue in Japanese. Baachan, who had first sat in her chair like a limp doll as a sign of her nonviolent protest, straightened up. Something that Yumi shared had caught her interest.

Court finally interrupted and turned to Baachan. "What she saying?"

"Your papa was a GI, American soldier. Ova in Marshall Islands. She didn't know him long. Apparently he was married when they got together."

Marshall Islands—a college classmate had been from those islands, halfway between here and the Philippines. I'd watched some documentary on the Marshall Islands and knew the US government had done some nuclear tests there.

"So I'm part Marshallese and part haole?"

Baachan said a few words to Yumi and she answered: "Got some Japanese blood in you too. Dat where the Yumi name come from."

"I'm confused," I said. "I thought Yumi was from Japan."

Baachan consulted with Yumi, who shook her head.

"She married a Japanese fella. That marriage didn't work out, but she stayed in Japan. Dat why she a Hara. Maiden name was Gasper."

I could tell that Court was soaking all this information in. All these separate threads braided together to be part of her DNA.

Yumi patted her own stomach, connecting with Court's pregnancy. "How long?" she asked in English.

Court rubbed her ridiculously swollen belly. Her legs and arms had remained thin as usual, so from the back she didn't even appear pregnant. Her side profile told another story altogether. "The baby is due in a few weeks." She made a peace sign with her fingers. "Two weeks," she said slowly.

Yumi sat back in her folding chair, a look of contentment on her face. She was going to be a grandmother.

Court's face relaxed too, looking like herself in the *before* times.

A car pulled into the lot, and I leaned back in my chair enough to see the back of a paneled station wagon from the 1970s. Ohmygoodness. The Lee-mobile.

I leaned forward to see who was heading into the shop. Both Mr. and Mrs. Lee. We were going to get the full-action reveal. I tightened my fists and tried to prepare myself for what was about to transpire.

Mrs. Lee entered first, her hair again perfectly coiffed in a Mad Man–era updo. She was carrying one of those reusable bags from Oʻahu's Foodland. She blinked hard, trying to absorb what was right in front of her. Her eyes locked onto the figure of Yumi Hara and she dropped her bag. Even Baachan looked scared.

"Chungmi, just don't stand there. I have junk in my hands." Mr. Lee stood behind her and then, exasperated, hurried to the counter to deposit a moving box he had been carrying. He turned to the table and finally noticed that we were also in the room. "Oh, you all here. Howzit, everyone?"

His face, unlike Mrs. Lee's, remained unchanged as he quickly gazed at Yumi. He had no idea who she was.

Court pushed herself up from her chair and, pressing her left hand into her back, gestured toward Mrs. Lee. "Did you know she was my mother?"

Mr. Lee caught on that something was very amiss. "Eh, what's going on?" His head went from his daughter to his wife and finally to Yumi. "Who dis?"

"Was I really left at the firehouse?" Court focused now on her father. "Dad, tell me the truth. Did you get me from DCFS?"

"Why all dis talk now?" Mr. Lee resembled a caged animal seeking escape.

"Is dis my bio mom or not?" She pointed at Yumi.

Mr. Lee stared at Mrs. Lee, whose body was sagging like a marionette puppet. "Chungmi, you tellin' me. . . ."

"Help her, Leilani," Baachan ordered, and I pulled out another folding chair for Mrs. Lee. Baachan always acted more like a grownup around women like Mrs. Lee.

Yumi also acted different around Mrs. Lee. It was obvious that they'd talked before.

I also unfolded a chair for Mr. Lee, who sat closest to the open door. He looked like someone had punched him in the face. I rushed to give him a cup of water. After he took a long sip, he started to talk story. "We tried everything. Looked into adopting from Korea and China. Went into Fost-Adopt training. Nothing was quite right. Or *we* weren't quite right. And then from some vet friends in Honolulu, I heard about Garvin Washburne."

"Washburne," I murmured.

"He was the attorney who was going to solve all our adoption problems. He knew about pregnant women on the Marshall Islands. They weren't married. They needed help. We paid him, and in three months' time we got Court."

"Why lie about it, Dad?" Court asked. "Why the stories about the firehouse?"

"When you were about five, we started hearing stories from other people who'd adopted from Washburne. That the birth mothers hadn't always agreed to adoption. I called him to try to find out details about your situation, Court. He told me not to worry, it was all legit. To just go along with our lives. But he said for your sake, Court, maybe I shouldn't tell you that your mother came from the Marshall Islands."

"And you just went along with it." A look of disgust spread over Court's face. "I can't believe it."

"You were our entire life," Mrs. Lee finally spoke. Her voice was soft, softer than I remember ever hearing it. "I loved you with every breath. I could not lose you."

Court furiously rubbed her belly as if it were a genie's lamp, able to grant her a magic wish.

Yumi stood up and bowed deeply toward Mrs. Lee. "*Domo arigato gozaimasu.*" She repeated the same thing to Mr. Lee.

I glanced at Baachan.

"She's giving the Lees her mahalo." Baachan explained what I had figured out on my own.

Court's chest started to expand, and I recognized her struggle to breathe. She was starting to have a panic attack.

"Let's take a break," I said, and rose to help her out of Lee's.

Outside, the sun was shining, a contrast to the gloominess inside the flower shop.

"Leilani, you have to do something." Sophie ran to my side from the picnic tables. She had obviously been waiting for me to emerge from Lee's.

"Can't you see that Auntie Court not feelin' well?"

"Oh, sorry, Auntie Court."

Court attempted to smile, but it ended up being more of a grimace. Sophie remained outside as we went into Santiago's.

I sat Court down and massaged her bony back. "You want an ice?" I offered.

"I don't want a damn ice," she snapped. I recalled Pekelo's account of Court throwing things, and I checked to make sure nothing dangerous was within her reach. She rubbed her eyes and took some deep breaths. "I'm sorry. I don't mean to take dis out on you."

Once her breathing returned to normal, I brought her a paper cup of water. She nodded thanks and took a dainty sip.

"How could my parents do dis to me? Lie for all those years?"

I sat back down at our card table. "It sounds like they were desperate. Maybe knew they didn't do everyting right. They didn't want to lose you. Either physically or emotionally."

"They were dead wrong. I have a right to know where I came from."

I couldn't argue with that.

"And what if I was taken without my bio mother's permission?"

I had been thinking the same thing. "All I know is that this Washburne is a bad man. He isn't to be trusted."

"This changes everyting, you know. All dis time, I've been thinking about not being loved or wanted."

"Court, you know that we love you!"

"I know *you* do. But my bio parents. The woman who gave birth to me. Being pregnant makes me think about it even mo'. Like how she could give me up li'dat."

After all our years as friends, I'd had no idea that Court was struggling with feelings of insecurity and a lack of self-worth. She had a naturally sunny, optimistic personality. I was the dark one, the needy friend. Perhaps I had sucked up all the darkness, not leaving any room for her to sit in her sadness and anger.

"But now hearin' that maybe she didn't give me up so easy. It's awful, Leilani, but a part of me feels happy. That she did want me. She just didn't have enough power to fight for me."

"For her to come all dis way to find you is someting, fo' sure."

We sat in the pureness of that truth for a while until I noticed Sophie standing in the shack's doorway, her leg shaking as if she needed to go shi-shi.

"What?!" I was so annoyed.

"I'll be okay, Leilani," Court said. "Find out what she wants. I'm going to lie down a bit at Books and Suds." Sean had set up a cot in his empty storefront for anyone who needed to take a nap during the day.

I went outside. "What?" I repeated, but a lot less aggressively.

Sophie didn't waste any time. "Ro's mom. DCFS picked up Ro. She's going in for foster care." She searched my face for the same level of indignation as hers. I never could hide my true feelings. "You called them." Her accusation felt red-hot.

"Sophie, I had to. This was way beyond us. You yourself said you didn't trust her mother's boyfriend."

She didn't want to hear my explanations. "I hate you! You're a loser," she spit out. "You're twenty-five and still living at home. Couldn't make it on the Mainland, so now we're stuck with you."

Okay, so she was going there.

"You're a scaredy-cat. A coward. A crybaby."

Normally I would have lashed out in anger, but I realized that Sophie was hurting. I was hurting too. "I wanted to help her, Sophie. Really I did. But what can we do?"

"We can be her foster family."

The procedures of the foster-care system were not new to me. Mom had actually looked into fostering after Emily and I left for college on the Mainland. This was before her MS diagnosis, when she was feeling the effects of her nest being emptied. She'd called me in Seattle to make sure it would be okay if our room was given over to a new child, at least for a little while until the kid got adopted.

"Ro would need her own room. She can't be sleeping in a tent in the backyard."

"So you not going to do anyting."

Doing nothing for once would be so glorious. To lie on the white sands underneath a palm tree with a piña colada at my side like the tourists did. For me, doing nothing was my idea of heaven.

"I didn't say that."

"You help when it's *your* friend."

"Ah—" I couldn't argue with that. These past few days, I'd been obsessing over Court and the mysterious mermaid woman.

Sophie stalked off toward the beach. The ocean would calm her nerves.

I felt like my shoulder blades had been replaced with metal rods. Those "girl power" slogans were bullshit. None of us Santiago girls felt empowered right now, except for maybe my mother, who was sewing masks like nobody's business.

Before checking on Court, I stuck my head into Lee's. The chairs around the work table were empty. "Where's everyone?" I asked Baachan, who was sitting by herself at the picnic table.

"Pau," she said. "Mrs. Lee wasn't feeling good, so Mr. Lee took her home."

"And Yumi?"

"She left."

"She *left*?!" Whatthehell?

"Some boy walking around the parking lot scare her away."

"What boy?"

Baachan sucked on her dentures before speaking. "You know, the Nakayama boy. Drives around in an ambulance."

Rocket Nakayama? "Yah, he come with other paramedics to help Yumi." Wait a minute, hadn't Baachan mentioned him earlier? "Didn't you say Washburne represented him in court?"

"Had some drug problems, but he turned tings around. Good ting dat lawyer got him off."

I had gone to school with Rocket since kindergarten. He was shaped like his name—thin and straight, with hardly any hips and shoulders to speak of. He could also be fiery and explosive like his name. He'd been a wisp of a boy in grade school. He was the one that everyone aimed for in dodgeball. But after high school, he began to lift weights and put some lean muscle on his thin frame. I heard he was heavy into online gambling.

"When she saw him, she jumped outta her skin," Baachan said.

Had Rocket done something to her in the hospital?

Baachan continued. "My friend dropped off some fabric for your madda. I turn my back for a second and she was gone."

Oh, fabric. Dammit. In all the excitement, I had forgotten about Dad's request. I'd have to take care of that before I chased after Yumi. I checked my phone to see if the Fed Ex offices were open on Sunday. Nope. I was afraid of that. I was able to locate an inter-island cargo service. I'd just have to get the package to the Līhu'e Airport by seven tonight.

I went into Killer Wave's storage unit, where, next to a new shipment of surf wax, I found the fabric swatches. The designs were an improvement over the urban-graffiti ones that my father first had produced. These were more traditional—a yellow hibiscus flower, an image of King Kamehameha, and a rooster that resembled Jimin (but then I guess all roosters pretty much look alike). I could see how both old-time kama'āina and tourists would take a liking to them. I stuffed the swatches into a big padded envelope, ran out of the shop, and jumped into the Fiesta.

Sophie's words sunk in deeper as I drove. I *was* kind of a loser. But I was too weary to care.

Finding the counter for the cargo service was easy. I felt a sense of accomplishment—maybe not so much like a loser—as the clerk printed out a computerized sticker with Dad's friend's address in O'ahu and stuck it on the envelope of swatches. Everything in that office was ordered and pristine, not like my everyday life at Waimea Junction. I made a quick stop in the airport, which seemed a lot busier than in the early months of the pandemic. Mainland visitors had Kaua'i fever. I just hoped they respected the land as much as we all had these past few months. Although it would have been close to impossible to spot Yumi in the crowd, I searched nonetheless. No sign of her.

I didn't see her hitchhiking along the highway either. Mama Liu, our local taxi driver, or one of the few Ubers on the island most likely took her to her next destination. But where? Maybe the guy who'd made her flee could provide some answers.

When I arrived at the hospital, I saw the paramedic's ambulance parked deep inside the parking lot. I still had my blue paper gown in the car in case I needed to sneak back into the hospital, but it turned out I didn't need to.

Back in high school, I remembered, Rocket had been a person of addictions. His eyes were constantly bloodshot from the weed he smoked in between periods. And now, leaning against the ambulance, he was taking puffs from a vape pen. As I approached him, I was bathed in the nauseating sweetness of raspberry smoke.

Rocket barely took a break from sucking on his vape. "Eh, howzit?"

"My baachan said she saw you at the Junction a few hours ago."

"Didn't think she'd remember me." Rocket was pretty forgettable, but Baachan never forgot a face, especially one who might be trouble.

"So what were you doing at Santiago's?"

"Just seeing if I could grab an ice."

"You know we've been closed."

Rocket shook his head. "Hard to keep track. Things change every day."

"Your madda doin' okay?"

Rocket was surprised that I recalled his mother. He and I had both been regulars in the principal's office, and I recalled her harried figure bursting in from her job managing a dental office in Waimea.

"Her arthritis acting up, so she retired last year."

"Give her my regards." Mrs. Nakayama came around Santiago's now and then in the *before* times. She went nostalgic with ujikintoki, matcha with azuki beans on the side. She had gone to Japan a couple of times when she was a kid, and her grandmother had bought her that in Hiroshima's cafes.

Rocket's face softened, and he lowered his vape.

"Hey, it's good you became a paramedic," I said. "Everyone's proud of you."

"Bullshit."

"Yeah, even your madda say dat when she come around for an ice." Of course, I would be the first to say it, and she just nodded in agreement. But that was as good as saying it, wasn't it?

Feeling that I had adequately buttered him up, I launched into the real reason I'd come to see him. "So, you were there to take Yumi Hara to the hospital."

Rocket cringed for a second, enough for me to know that Yumi's name meant something to him.

"Yeah, what about it?"

"Seems like she knows you."

"How's dat? I haven't said two words to her."

"But you talking about her, right? Lemme guess—to Garvin Washburne."

Rocket let out some dry laughs. It almost sounded like he was coughing.

"How much money is he giving you?"

"Dat's none of your business."

"But Yumi Hara *is* my business."

"She's just a two-bit tour agent from Japan."

"She's like family." I wasn't lying at that point. Court was like my fourth sister, and if Yumi was her bio mom, she had joined our circle.

Rocket studied my face, probably to look for signs that I was lying. He was supporting his single mom, and I knew family meant everything to him. "I know notting, Leilani."

"Yeah?"

"Yeah."

I didn't believe him for a second. He had the same look on his face as our small-kid times, when he'd pull Court's hair hard but deny it to the teacher. "By the way, is Taiji Wong still your best friend?" I had forgotten until now. I could picture them in high school, always sitting underneath the same banyan tree during lunch.

"We keep in touch. He's overseas with the Navy."

"I heard he has a motorcycle."

Rocket's face grew pale and his right eye twitched. "What about it?"

"Notting. A motorcycle the oddah day make me lose my malasada."

Rocket pressed his face in a smile. He thought I was joking.

"No laughing matter," I told him. "It was one damn good malasada."

Monday

Chapter Thirteen

COURT WAS THE SUGAR to my salt. Since small-kid time we'd known of each other because of our respective family businesses next to each other. Later our friendship was forged on the lawn of our junior high school campus. She'd been home-schooled until sixth grade and was new to all the mean girl factions at school. People were chill and friendly enough in person, but when you turned your back, the knives came out.

I wanted her to go away, but she stayed by my side. She could have easily joined the circle of the kawaii, the popular girls, the thin ones who actually brushed their hair in the morning. I'm not sure what she saw in me, but I think she appreciated that I wouldn't talk around something. In that way, I am my father's daughter. I can't make my words pretty.

But like they say, don't judge a book by its cover. I'm really mushier than I'd like to admit, while Court can be like iron beneath her outwardly sunny persona. Before, I thought it was because she'd been abandoned at a firehouse and a part of her knew that she'd have to rely on her inner strength to make it in this world. But after meeting Yumi, I was starting to wonder whether Court hadn't inherited some of her doggedness.

So when I saw Court waiting for me on the porch at my family's house, her swollen ankles splayed out and a duffel bag at her side, I wasn't surprised.

"I need you to take me to Hanalei," she announced. "I need to talk to Kelly to find out what he did or didn't know."

I didn't bother to argue with her. I went inside to tell Mom and grab clean underwear and a T-shirt. The way our life was going, I had to be prepared for anything. And it would be good to get a break from Sophie's anger. I had noticed that she left the living room the minute she saw me.

Court filled me in on the details as I drove. It turned out that Yumi had come to pick up the lei early that Sunday morning before I'd arrived to help out. Only Mrs. Lee had been there. Her elders had grown up under Japanese rule, so Mrs. Lee had picked up some Japanese, enough to make everyday conversation. Yumi knew who she was and sprung the big revelation: she was Court's bio mother.

"Mom was shocked. She wanted to go home, but she knew that you were coming to help with some leis."

I hadn't sensed that anything was wrong with Mrs. Lee, but then, she had the ultimate poker face.

"She said notting to me while Yumi was in that coma." Court's voice was bitter. "What if she'd died?"

"Did she tell you how they came to adopt you?"

"They bought me from that attorney. Garvin Washburne."

My stomach twisted into knots. "Whatchu mean, 'bought'?"

"They went to Garvin for help, and he told them he knew of mothers who were giving up their babies. For a price. He assured them that it was all legal."

"But it wasn't."

"That part I'm not sure of. That's why we need to find Yumi too. Your baachan told me she disappeared."

"She probably heading back to her Airbnb."

"That's what I figured too."

While we were waiting at a stoplight in Kapaʻa, I located the frat house address and clicked on that to replace Uncle Rick's address.

"So many businesses closed." Court hadn't traveled much out of Waimea, either, and the sight of so many shuttered stores was new to her.

I opened the side windows so the ocean air could blow away our melancholy. Nature was the only thing that could truly heal us.

I had Court call Uncle Rick as I drove through Princeville. "He's in Līhuʻe, but says that the boys are probably still at work."

I nodded. I was thankful that I had filled the gas tank when I went to the airport. It certainly looked like I'd be doing my share of driving today.

I turned on the quiet cul-de-sac in Hanalei where Yumi's Airbnb was located.

"Yumi staying at a high-tone place."

"Yeah, she must be pretty successful as a travel agent," Court revealed.

"I wanted to be a travel agent once."

"I nevah know dat."

"Yah, I nevah tell nobody. But I thought it would be fun to travel some. Before I settled down and had babies."

We parked in front of the Airbnb. The air here was so soft and clean; my lungs felt as if they were being purified. Again, like before, there were no cars parked on the street. It was a ghost neighborhood. I gazed at the sky for any drone sightings, but only a few geese flew by.

I went to the passenger's side and extended my hand to pull Court out of her seat. Even though her due date wasn't for a couple of weeks, she looked like she was going to burst any second. The skin on her thin body didn't seem like it had any more excess to accommodate this baby.

I rapped on the front door as we stood on the porch. No response.

"The bell, Leilani." Court jabbed at the doorbell; it worked, because we heard it. No Yumi.

"Yumi. It's me, Court." Quiet as a mouse.

"Wait here," I said. I walked through the tall grasses to get access to the back. The large windows revealed a staid living room and kitchen. All the furniture seemed undisturbed since I'd trespassed inside on Wednesday. "Yumi," I called out. Remembering my elementary Japanese, I said, "Yumi-*san*," just to be a little more polite. I heard nothing. Only the trickling of water from the fountain in the garden.

I traipsed again through the foliage to return to the front. "She's not here," I said.

"Then where is she?"

"Maybe she's on her way?" I had no idea how she was able to find transportation out of Waimea. Ride-share services were limited on Kaua'i anyway, and during the pandemic they were pretty much nonexistent.

"I'm so mad at Mom. Why did she keep all this information from me? And now that Yumi has disappeared, I'll nevah get any answers."

"We'll find her," I said.

Dejected, we returned to the Ford.

Court looked up the kalo farm and plugged it into my phone. We couldn't imagine a world without GPS. How had my parents gotten around?

The kalo farm was located in a part of Hanalei featured in all the tourist advertisements, in a valley surrounded by craggy green mountain peaks. In the early morning, a mist typically fell over the patchwork of green kalo fields.

Both Kelly and Pekelo were bent over in the kalo fields, hacking away at the intertwined and stubborn roots of the yam.

"Kelly! Kelly!" Court screamed from the edge of her fields. Her voice was so thin that the sounds she expelled disappeared into the horizon.

"Eh, Kelly!" I bellowed. I could get my voice a couple octaves lower than Court, but to no avail. Both of them had earbuds in their ears, and rap was usually their music of choice.

Court kicked off her slippah and started walking in the wet muck.

"Stop! You gonna fall on your okole!" Or, worse, her belly. I forced her to stay on land as I made my way through the goopy mud. It actually felt good on the soles of my feet and my toes, but the soil was leaving a terrible residue on my calves and thighs. I regretted not bringing a clean pair of shorts with me.

I was about four feet from the brothers when I tried again. "Hey, Kelly!"

"Oh, whatchu doing here?" Kelly fiddled with his phone with the side of his hand to turn off his tunes. He looked past me toward the mud bank where Court was standing.

"Is she okay?"

"She's fine. Kind of. I mean, her body is fine."

Kelly's face fell. "She found out who that lady was." He already knew.

"Uh-huh. She's out for blood. You're next."

Pekelo, by this time, had stopped working and pulled out his earbuds. Kelly must have told him about everything, because he stuffed his buds back in and resumed hacking the roots with his machete.

Kelly and I trudged back to dry land. A few brown ducks and a black coot glided through the low water in the irrigation ditches.

"Eh," he greeted Court, and she gave him stink eye in return. He placed his machete on a safe spot on the ground and attempted to brush the coat of mud from his hands.

"Well, did you know?" Court's fists rested on her still-slim hips.

He nodded. "She called the shop. Or rather dis oddah lady wen call for her. When I told her I was Court's husband, she started saying that she was with the woman who was your real mom. I told her no come around. That she was not welcome."

Court shook her head. "How could you?"

"I just wanted to protect you."

"By keeping my own madda away from me?"

"You have a mom. A mom that took care of you ever since you were abandoned at that firehouse."

"Ah, maybe I wasn't abandoned like dat!"

"Whatchu mean?"

As we walked back to the main building, Court explained how the Lees had worked with an attorney to get her.

"I no get it. Why dey nevah tell you dat from da beginning?"

"There's someting more behind it. I can feel it in my bones."

That saying sounded funny coming from Court, but I felt it too.

The tension between the newlyweds was breaking, and I lagged a little behind so they could have a little privacy.

"We're going to be parents. We need to be on the same side," Court was imploring Kelly.

He nodded and put his dirty arm around Court's shoulders. None of us cared about some mud.

"Well, what I said didn't stop your bio mom from coming around again. She's pretty hard head. Like someone else I know."

Court wasn't in the mood to kid around. "And the shop. It's going under. No one bothered to tell me dat, either. You and my parents, just because I have another life inside of me, you tink that I can't tink."

Kelly hung his head down. He knew he'd done wrong. The thing about him, though, was that he wasn't too proud to be remorseful. I couldn't say the same thing about his older brother.

Once we reached the farm's office, Kelly turned toward me. "You can wash up at the office," he told me, referring to our dirty feet and calves. I then recalled a detail from his confession.

"You said you spoke to a lady who called for Yumi Hara. You know her name?"

"Washburne. Virginia Washburne. She kept saying her name like it was going to make me jump. It was only after her ex-husband killed that nurse at Sammie's place that I found out who she was."

Court looked up to me. "Maybe you can find out more information from dis Washburne lady?"

Oh my God, did everyone think I was the island's resident PI now? Yet I didn't hate the title. At least I was good at something.

It wasn't difficult for me to locate Virginia Washburne's residence. It was known to everyone in the area. I asked Kelly about Mrs. Washburne as I was hosing down my feet in the communal washroom, and the office worker started piping in with an answer.

"It's ova dere by Hanalei Park on Weke Road. Famous for lights every Christmas."

"Oh, the Washburne house, yah?" the secretary chimed in.

Kelly, meanwhile, was attempting to patch up his relationship with the mother of his future child. I didn't want to interrupt their quiet conversation, and after I dried my feet with a towel kindly provided to me by the secretary I texted both of them that I'd see them back at Uncle Rick's house.

Once I returned to the Ford, I googled Virginia Washburne and Kaua'i and finally came up with an address. Nothing was secret anymore, no matter how much you sought to hide your address. With the location on Google Maps, I went north on Weke Road and found the house in a few seconds. It was a beautiful white two-story wood structure with an expansive side veranda. On the front lawn were probably a hundred carved pumpkins precisely lined up in ten rows. It must have been a sight at night with all the candles lit. It seemed clear that Virginia Washburne was big on holidays and also had a lot of time on her hands.

The house had an open layout, with an outdoor dining table on the ground floor. An older haole woman was sitting there reading with a wine glass beside her as I walked up the driveway. She must have not been fully absorbed in her reading, because she immediately spotted me. Putting down her book, she fastened her mask and met me halfway.

"Hi, I'm Leilani Santiago. I've never met you. But I saw you. At the protest at the frat house."

"You want to sit down?" Virginia gestured toward the table in the open area. "No walls, good ventilation."

Her house looked straight out of a luxury magazine, and I couldn't refuse. As I approached, she retrieved a bottle of wine from an adjoining room.

"Would you like a glass? Pineapple wine from Maui."

Why not? I nodded my head. D-man said he'd rather be shot than offer pineapple wine at his bar, but I'd always wanted to try it.

She poured the wine as I took my seat in a teak chair. I felt like I was in the middle of a TV show, without all the cameras. I pulled down my mask to drink. The wine, which was chilled, was sweet, but not like Dole syrup. It definitely provided a blast of pineapple, so refreshing and a reminder of summer.

"You have a lot of pumpkins," I commented after pulling up my mask.

"Halloween is my favorite holiday after Christmas. Too bad I won't have any trick-or-treaters this year."

I'd forgotten all about such things, and Dani hadn't brought it up. Maybe that was my bad. It might be fun to make Waimea Junction into a haunted house on October 31. No, strike that. I could picture all those young ones crowded into our space. Better to leave Halloween as a flat balloon than blow any air into it.

"So," Virginia finally said. "You didn't come here to drink pineapple wine."

"No," I admitted, tracing my index finger around the base of my glass. "I heard that you've been helping Yumi Hara."

"How is she? Do you know where she is? I've been calling the hospital regularly to see how she's doing; and the last time I called, I heard she'd checked out."

So it was confirmed by the woman herself: Virginia Washburne was the regular caller. Well, that solved that mystery.

"It turns out she's my best friend's birth mother," I said.

"Oh, you're Courtney Lee's friend. Does Courtney know? Her husband wasn't that cooperative. But Yumi told me that wasn't going to stop her." I was amazed at how much this chatty woman knew about the situation. If I had found her earlier, it would have saved me a lot of time.

"How did you meet her?"

"She came to our ... well, my house. She wanted to speak to Garvin. I told her we were divorcing."

"You know Japanese?"

"I was a flight attendant in a former life." She took a big sip of her wine. "That's actually how I met Garvin. Been keeping up my language skills. In Hawai'i, not so hard." Virginia's aging skin was shriveled and skin-damaged, but her mind was razor sharp. "I miss talking to people; so when she came by, we sat outside and chatted. I mentioned my own children and I asked if she had any. She told me only one. And that she was looking for her. Garvin's old secretary was even helping her for a while."

A former secretary? I felt my heart skip a beat. Maybe she could provide us with more answers.

"It just so happens that I had files from thirty years ago in the garage. Garvin was supposed to come and pick them up at some point. That was before the pandemic." A couple of ducks shuffled across Virginia's lawn in between the rows of jack-o'-lanterns.

"So I looked up Yumi Hara—well, she was Yumi Gasper back then. And there it was. Her daughter had been adopted by a couple in Waimea, here on Kaua'i. I even had an address. Who knows, I told her. People here don't move around much. Maybe they're even at the same address."

"You called the flower shop."

"Yes, I spoke to Courtney's husband. I probably said too much, because he totally shut down the conversation. Yumi figured that she better speak to Courtney face-to-face."

I wondered if Mrs. Washburne was releasing this rush of information because she'd been so isolated during the pandemic. I had opened a door and now was deluged with more than I expected. "My husband is a control freak," she continued. "I thought maybe if we moved to Kaua'i, the slower pace would help our marriage. But he managed instead to find a new woman. A month ago, he told me that she's pregnant. He's seventy years old and going to be a father again. Have you ever heard of anything so ridiculous?"

The old woman was furious. That anger must have fueled her desire to help Yumi. Maybe I could use that energy to help myself. "Do you think I can take a look at those files right now?"

Virginia gave me a long look-over. I wasn't sure if what I was asking her to do was legal. It certainly wasn't ethical. But she was going to be rid of Garvin Washburne soon. What did it matter?

The garage was big enough to hold three cars. The file boxes were arranged by year and then alphabetically. Virginia stayed with me in the garage for only a few minutes before she became bored and returned to her house. I looked up Ted's last name on one of Taylor's news stories on the internet. Ted Rumpf. I started with the oldest files from thirty years ago. I was striking out every year. I was getting paper cuts on practically every finger. Office work was obviously not for me—too dangerous. Finally, in the twenty-year-old files, I found it. Stanley and Glory Rumpf. That had to be Ted's parents. My fingers shook as I removed the file from the box. I sat on the garage floor, which was cleaner than my bedroom one, and carefully opened the manila folder. There was biographical information on the adoptive parents, including a photo of Ted's parents. Stanley was heavy, with red hair and a slight mustache, and the mother, Glory, had one of those smiles that you instantly trusted. One son, Ted, was mentioned. He'd been four years old when the couple contacted Washburne about adopting another child.

I went to the next packet of information. A metal clip held various forms. Typed was a woman's name and an address in the Marshall Islands. And then a photo of a three-month-old baby.

Ted's adoptive little sister and her bio mother were from the Marshall Islands. This was the link between Ted, Court, and Washburne.

"Did you find what you were looking for?" Virginia came into the garage with another glass of wine.

I quickly closed the file and put it back in the box. I didn't even bother taking photos of what I'd seen. I didn't think it was my place. I wanted confirmation of a link between Garvin and Ted, and I'd seen that link with my own eyes. That was good enough.

"Did Yumi tell you why she gave up her baby?" I asked.

"She told me it wasn't her choice. That she was bamboozled. She was too young to understand everything that was happening. She's regretted what she did for her whole life." She took another sip of her wine, spilling some drops on the garage floor. She didn't seem to notice. "It was a godsend when Garvin's secretary contacted her out of the blue. Alice said she'd been searching for Yumi—she wanted to come clean about how Garvin handled these adoptions from the Marshall Islands."

Wow. What a story. Taylor could really sink her journalistic fangs into this. "Do you think you can give me the old secretary's contact information?"

"Oh, dear, I wish I could. She passed away in an awful car accident in Honolulu. Can you believe that? In the middle of a pandemic."

This whole situation was making me sick to my stomach. It sounded like Garvin Washburne had been involved in baby trafficking, at least a couple of decades ago. That's how Ted's adoptive sister had come into his family. And Courtney to the Lees.

I was getting frightened for Yumi. If Washburne had shot Ted dead and his secretary had been killed in a mysterious car crash, there was no telling what he'd do to Yumi. She'd been safer in the hospital than in the wilds of Kaua'i.

After thanking Virginia for her help, I drove to Yumi's Airbnb to see if she was there. Again the cul-de-sac was deserted and no cars were parked either in the driveway or on the street.

"Yumi! Yumi! It's me, Leilani." It dawned on me that she probably didn't even know my name. "Court's friend. *Tomodachi.*" Friend.

Nothing.

I went back to the car and found an old drugstore receipt that was about a foot long. On the back of it I wrote my name and phone number, asking her to call me. I also included Uncle Rick's address in case she had problems making a phone call. After scribbling that information, I stuffed the folded receipt in the doorjamb.

I couldn't remember if there was a landline in the Airbnb. Now that cell phones were everywhere, hotels and vacation rentals didn't have phones in rooms anymore. I'd heard that Japanese visitors couldn't call or text with their cell phones in the US without signing on to an American service. But there was still the internet. I hated social media, but I'd been getting more involved with Santiago's Shave Ice Facebook page, Twitter feed, and Instagram account. They were all languishing during the pandemic, but my small-business friends had been pushing me to post inspirational memes against ocean backgrounds. They obviously didn't know me that well.

I tried to find Yumi Hara on Facebook, Twitter, and Instagram. There were some Yumi Haras; but judging by their profile pics and locations, they weren't the Yumi Hara I was looking for.

It dawned on me that I was searching in English—how the hell to write Yumi Hara in Japanese? I knew that in Japanese, the last names came first, so I googled "Hara and Japanese name." I found a kanji, copied it and pasted it in my search bar for Facebook. Now for Yumi. That had a lot more options. I attempted all sorts of combinations. No one who looked like our Yumi.

From my Japanese classes long ago, I remembered a few letters in the Japanese phonetic alphabet. There were two sets, katakana and hiragana. I tried both of those, and yaass! The hiragana "Yumi" hit gold.

There in the profile circle was her face, shaded by a visor. Her cover photo was of a white sandy beach. I wondered if it could be on the Marshall Islands.

Her posts were set to private, only visible to her friends, but I could send her a message. I knew the chances were close to nil that she'd see it, but I had to at least try. It was better than doing nothing.

Yumi, it's Leilani Santiago, Courtney's friend. I wanted to keep talking to you.

And I left my cell phone number.

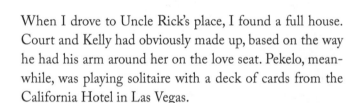

When I drove to Uncle Rick's place, I found a full house. Court and Kelly had obviously made up, based on the way he had his arm around her on the love seat. Pekelo, meanwhile, was playing solitaire with a deck of cards from the California Hotel in Las Vegas.

"So, were you able to talk to Washburne's ex-wife?" Kelly asked.

I wasn't sure why I hesitated. But to see my pregnant BFF and her husband finally happy together made me hold my tongue. Why pull Court into danger at a time like this? She'd already met her bio mom and could learn more details about her adoption later from Mr. and Mrs. Lee. Did it matter how it all had gone down? Garvin Washburne was more powerful and influential than any of us. Our landlord, Sean Cohen, had pull in the tech world, but fighting against human trafficking was out of his purview. When we'd worked together to clear my father's name last year, I learned that he had an obsession that he inherited from his grandfather: to extinguish any forms of Nazism from the face of the earth. I'm sure that some of those skills could transfer to capture baby-traffickers, but Sean wasn't around to help. It would be up to me.

I shook my head and felt the heaviness of the room lift. That night we played Hearts and Crazy Eights while eating hurricane popcorn with kakimochi and furikake. We laughed and joked, for a few moments forgetting that a deadly pandemic had gripped the entire world.

Chapter Fourteen

IN SPITE OF ALL THE SUN that was streaming through the windows of Uncle Rick's house, I slept in until ten. Kelly and Pekelo had gone in to work, leaving Court on Rick's couch and me on the floor again, but this time on a plush air mattress that you inflated with your foot.

Rick had brought in some fresh eggs from his chicken coop and had made some coffee, incentive for me to finally wake up. Court, on the other hand, was snoring like a bear on the couch.

"You sleep okay?" Rick asked.

"Like a baby. Haven't slept this good in ages. Maybe before the pandemic."

We both should have been wearing masks in the house, but since our game night last night we felt a certain kind of intimacy. It wouldn't save us from the virus, of course, but I had temporarily pushed that fear aside.

"You want an omelet, loco moco?"

"You still have hot rice in the cooker?"

Rick gave me a thumbs-up. "Good idea," he said. He cracked two fresh eggs in a bowl, whisked them with a fork and then added a splash of shoyu. Using a shamoji, he placed mounds of hot rice into two chawan and then poured half of the egg-and-soy-sauce mixture in each.

I pulled out a pair of chopsticks from a beer stein that Rick kept on the kitchen table. "Dis tamago rice takes me back." I stabbed my chopsticks into the hot concoction and mixed it thoroughly before shoveling it into my mouth. I would occasionally eat a raw egg on rice in Seattle, but not nearly as often as I'd have liked, because it freaked out Travis too much.

Eating egg over rice with coffee didn't make for a good combination, so I finished my bowl before pouring myself a big mug of coffee.

"Dis from the Big Island? Kaʻu?" I asked. I picked up a certain nutty and citrus aftertaste in the brew, which was exquisite.

Rick showed me the package to confirm my guess.

"Uncle, you splurged. Expensive stuff! I dealt with them when Santiago's was open." That was the company with the cute sales rep.

"Have you thought about reopening?"

"I'm not sure. Will anyone come? Hardly any tourists."

"Still plenty of people who live here like shave ice too. Give them some sunshine in their life."

"Yeah." Yumi herself had wanted an old-school Japanese ice with condensed milk and azuki beans. For others, it was Dole whip. It was something to think about, for sure.

I got on the internet through my phone and connected to Facebook. Lo and behold, mixed in with multiple friend requests from middle-aged men on yachts and military uniforms was a reply from Yumi. She had written it only thirty minutes earlier.

HELP.

She also included the street address for her Airbnb.

What is going on? My fingers trembled as I wrote. Thank goodness for automatic spell-check.

I waited for about a minute. No response.

I gulped down my coffee, which had become lukewarm, but I wasn't going to waste one drop. "I have to go, Uncle Rick."

"Hot date?"

I wasn't in the mood for lame dad jokes and shook my head. I grabbed my keys and grabbed my Crocs from the front. "Where you going, Leilani?" Court had woken up, still in what she'd worn last night but nonetheless managing to look fresh as a daisy.

"Ah." I didn't have time to lie. "Yumi's Airbnb. I think she needs help."

"Well, I'm going."

"No. It may be dangerous."

"I'll drive, at least. I'll stay in the car. You'll need a wing woman."

It would help to have another person.

"She's my bio madda, Leilani. Mine." That sealed it.

"Well, hurry up, then."

We ran—well, I ran while Court super-waddled—to the minivan. I turned on Google Maps, and we silently let its robotic voice guide us. My heart was racing. I opened the van's glove compartment, searching for anything that I could possibly use as a weapon. Sadly, there was only the vehicle manual and car-insurance information.

"What are you looking for?" Court's swollen fingers were firmly around the steering wheel as she sped through the Hanalei streets.

"A pocketknife, or something else to defend myself."

As Court turned onto the street of Washburne's rental, I cursed.

"What?"

"That's Garvin Washburne's car."

"Are you sure?"

"Look at the license plate." WASHATTY1 on a maroon Lexus.

"Shit." Court never cursed, but now was a good time to do it.

I got out of the van and Court followed. "You said you were going to stay in the van." Above us was the buzzing of a drone.

She handed me a knife with a short blade and plastic yellow handle. A florist's knife for cutting stems. It was certainly better than nothing. I carefully placed it in my fanny pack. "You need me," she said.

"Okay, but—" I put my fingers to my lips to signal that we had to be stealthy. We tiptoed to the front door. I placed my ear to the door. I could hear a male voice talking. But not Yumi's.

"He's in there," Court hissed. "Should I call 911?"

I shook my head. It was too early. We didn't know what Washburne was doing in there.

We went through the side gate into the lush garden. We peeked through the kitchen window. Washburne was in there, pacing back and forth. I narrowed my eyes to focus. Dammit. That was a gun in his hand. Who the hell was he talking to? Was he on the phone? I whispered for Court to stay put while I inched forward to a low window. From there I saw Yumi, tied up to a chair with her mouth muzzled by a bandanna. I felt like I couldn't breathe. I fumbled for my phone and, attempting to hold it as steady as possible, snapped a few photos before sneaking back to Court. "Yumi's in there," I whispered while Airdropping her the photos of the captive Yumi. "Go back to the car and call 911."

Court stared at the photos I'd sent. "We have to go in there and save my madda."

"And have him shoot her? He has a gun. Best thing is to call the cops. And send those photos to Andy too."

Court relented and waddle-ran to make her phone call.

I knelt down and watched as Washburne questioned Yumi, or rather threatened her. I felt scared for her, true horror. Look what he had done to Ted. And his former secretary. He'd do anything to protect his reputation.

Washburne was using his litigious lawyer voice, loud enough that I could hear it from outside. "I know you speak some English, so don't play ignorant with me. You made a big mistake by coming here. You signed that paper giving up your rights. This whole thing was your decision. Not mine. Your daughter has had a wonderful life here with her adoptive parents. That's what you wanted, right? A better future for her."

Yumi's dark eyes burned. She obviously understood every word he was saying.

"So we are going to get that COVID test. And in three days you will go back to Japan."

Yumi shook her head.

"Listen, I don't want to hurt you. And I certainly don't want to hurt your daughter. She's having a baby, right?"

Yumi struggled with the restraints around her wrists and ankles. She was hopping mad. There was no way she was going to go quietly back to Japan.

I needed a diversion. A big one. I look up and saw a drone in the air. Could it be his?

I typed a message to Adam:

Ur drone above Hanalei now?

Adam responded immediately: *Sorry. Is it bothering someone?*

I pinpointed my location on Google Maps and sent it to him.

I need u to crash it into front window.

What?

Emergency.

I then texted him the photo of Yumi tied up, with Washburne's gun pointed at her.

Adam stopped texting—I hoped he was busy trying to position himself and his drone. I spent the next few minutes carefully removing the glass panels from that window. Fortunately, Washburne was still ranting and raving at Yumi, desperately trying to frighten her into returning to Japan. She wasn't agreeing to anything. I wished she'd just fake being compliant, but I guess that wasn't her style. I had to give her credit for her fighting spirit.

I, on the other hand, was a freaking mess. I was trying to create a way into the Airbnb as quickly as possible, but my hands were shaking like crazy. I almost dropped the third window panel, but I managed to steady my right hand just in time.

"Just nod that pretty head of yours. You *will* go back to Japan."

Yumi made unintelligible noises through the bandanna. I didn't think she was saying yes.

BANG!

Adam had come through. The drone crashing into the front window sounded like a small explosion. Glass shattered across the ceramic tile entry wall. Washburne cocked his gun and shielded himself behind a column next to the kitchen, craning his neck to see what had happened. When he opened the front door to see if someone was outside, I had my opportunity. I jumped through the open window and grabbed the florist's knife in my fanny pack. Yumi's eyes widened, and she gestured for me to cut her right hand free from the black duct tape. I did so, and she worked on her left hand while I cut the tape around her calves. I ripped off the tape, leaving red marks on her slender legs.

I pulled her up and, hand in hand, we were about to escape out the back door when I heard Washburne's voice. "Stop or I'll shoot."

Yumi's fingers were clammy and wet in mine. Washburne aimed his gun squarely at Yumi. "Why did you turn out to be such a thorn in my side?" he said to me. "It really didn't have to be like this. I was just giving couples what they wanted—a baby. What kind of future would these babies have from such a rinky-dink sinking island that probably won't exist by the twenty-second century? But no. You people had to make a fuss, twenty, thirty years later."

I could see the gears working in Washburne's brain. It was one thing to make a tourist from the Marshall Islands disappear; but me, a native of Kaua'i, with a whole community behind me? I would be harder to dispense of. I imagine that some kind of choreographed accident was called for.

He gestured for Yumi to sit back in the chair and ordered me to secure her legs and wrists again with the duct tape left on the dining room table. He had shot Ted in cold blood and he could easily do the same with Yumi. I first wrapped the tape loosely around Yumi's ankles, but Washburne checked and demanded that I do it tighter. *Where were the police?*

Once I was finished, Washburne motioned with his gun for me to follow him out the front door, which was ajar.

I shook my head and remained in the living room. I remembered watching an episode of *Law & Order* when somebody said that you never get into an assailant's car. Once you were taken to another location, you were dead meat.

"If you're going to shoot me, shoot me right here," I said. I was surprised at my voice, which came out clear and calm, nothing like the panic that I felt inside.

Yumi now was practically lifting herself in the chair in protest.

"You don't mean that." Washburne held the gun with both hands, positioning himself to shoot me right between the eyes. I was ready to duck and run, but deep inside I knew I couldn't outrun a bullet.

In my silent shock, I barely noticed a lithe figure approaching Washburne from behind. Court had taken hula lessons as a child. Even with her protruding stomach, her footsteps were graceful and, most importantly, soundless. A flurry of colors emerged above Washburne's head: magenta orchids, red carnations, green ti leaves, and brown kukui nuts. All strung on different lines of leis and all now wrapped around Washburne's neck. Tightening and strangling him. He lurched back in response, his eyes bulging and his mouth wide open. His gun dropped from his hand and clattered onto the ceramic floor.

I dove for the gun. Court had pulled Washburne down onto the floor, and his fists were tightened around the leis as he desperately tried to free himself.

I had never held a gun in my life. I tried to replicate what I'd seen my favorite detectives do on *Law & Order SVU*. "Stop moving," I screamed at Washburne. He kept struggling with Court, who was also on the ground, holding on to the leis for dear life.

"I said stop!" I didn't know what I was doing, only that my BFF who was ready to pop out a baby might get hurt.

I aimed the gun up at the ceiling and pressed down on the trigger with my two index fingers. A pop like a firecracker, and white pieces of the cathedral ceiling fell down into the kitchen.

Adam was in the doorway holding his drone. He obviously was in shock, because he wasn't moving.

"Help her!" I gestured toward Court, and he dragged her away from Washburne, who was attempting to free himself from all the leis that Court had used to entrap him.

"I said don't move."

The red carnations covered his eyes, so he couldn't see me; but from the sound of my voice, he realized I was serious, and he knew I had his gun. He raised his arms as he lay on the tile floor. Now that Court was safely outside, I was prepared to shoot him and stop the terror that he had inflicted on my friends and family.

Police squad cars braked in the middle of the cul-de-sac, and officers descended upon the Airbnb. Through the open front door, I could see Court flag them down and her telling them what had happened.

Andy, his gun cocked, ready for anything, was the first officer who appeared in the doorway. A line of others stood behind him.

"Leilani, everyting okay?"

I kept the gun on Washburne. "He was going to take me somewhere and get rid of me."

Washburne was smart enough to stay quiet.

"We have everyting under control now. Just put the gun down."

I felt the police presence in the room, and I knew they weren't playing around. I placed the gun on the floor and got up with my hands raised.

The next few moments flashed by. Andy led me out to the lawn, while other officers turned Washburne over and secured his hands with plastic ties. When they helped him to his feet, some of the leis remained awkwardly looped around his neck and shoulders, torn flowers falling to the ground as they led him to a squad car.

I had almost forgotten about Yumi. After sitting with Andy to give my side of the story, I saw her being led out of the house by a female cop.

"You finished with me?" I asked Andy.

"You'll have to come by headquarters to speak to the detectives."

Fine, fine. I was getting used to going to the police station by now.

I found Yumi with Court next to a wooden fence separating the Airbnb property from the next-door neighbor.

Yumi rushed over, wrapping her arms around my neck. Her embrace felt familiar. It felt like Court's.

I checked in with Court, who was standing awkwardly against the fence. "You okay?"

She shook her head and pointed to the front of her dress, which was wet.

"I think I'm going to have a baby."

"It's not supposed to happen like this." Court was distraught. She didn't want to go to the hospital in a patrol car. According to COVID rules, I couldn't go with her. She'd have to make this trek alone. At least Andy was driving her.

"It will be okay, Court." I tried to make my voice as bright as possible but was failing miserably. "Kelly will meet you there."

Court scrunched up her face as she was overcome by another contraction. Yumi was beside herself. I knew she wanted to dive into the back seat with Court, but their relationship was still distant and tenuous, although inside her slight body was the beating of a mother's heart.

The two of us stood there as Andy drove our girl out of the cul-de-sac, sirens screaming and lights flashing.

Yumi looked at me as if to say *What now?*

"We, uh, go. To friend's house. Uncle Rick."

Yumi frowned as she tried to follow my weak efforts to communicate in broken English.

I recalled how Sophie had been nagging me about Google Translate and found the app already loaded on my phone. I experimented with it a few times until Yumi interrupted: "*Umi.*"

That much Japanese I knew without using Google Translate. She wanted to go to the beach.

We sat on the Hanalei Bay shore, much like I had done with Court some days ago in Waimea Bay. The view of the ocean from the sands of Hanalei was completely different from back home. In Waimea, there were hardly any waves. The sky filled the horizon. It was usually sunny, and there was a stillness that calmed me. Here, our surroundings were wet, green, and lush, as if the earth was giving us a sloppy kiss, and the waves out on the bay were big. The concrete pier led to a canopy in the distance.

Yumi explained that Court had always been on her mind. There hadn't been a day in which she didn't think of her. My eyes became wet as I thought of the prayers and thoughts that her mother had been releasing for my BFF over the Pacific Ocean.

"Court is a special person," I said into the phone, letting Google Translate do its work.

Yumi frowned in confusion. "*Sanbansho?*"

I looked at the screen. The name, Court, was translated into "courthouse" in Japanese.

I tried it again. "Court-*san* is a special person."

This time the translation made sense, because Yumi was smiling.

Holding my phone to her masked mouth, she began to talk slowly in Japanese. The Google female voice did a pretty good job of translating her story. There were some odd words inserted here and there, but I was able to follow along.

Yumi had begun actively searching for Court after her divorce. She'd never told her husband about having a daughter. It was this concealment that maybe had destroyed the relationship. Some days she'd be paralyzed by depression. Her husband hadn't known what to do. If only she had shared with him what had been consuming her, maybe the marriage could have been saved.

She'd even considered taking her own life. I let the robotic voice sink in deep. "I thought I would commit suicide."

And then, out of the blue, she received a call at work. From a strange white woman from America. An older lady named Alice Burton. She explained that she worked for an attorney, Garvin Washburne.

Yumi didn't know the name of the attorney who had taken her baby. It was only supposed to be for a limited time, nothing permanent. Yes, she had been terribly naïve, but she was only twenty years old and scared.

She had been exchanging emails regularly with Alice. Then the exchanges stopped.

"I thought I had to go to Hawaiʻi even if I had a pandemic," the Google female translator said. Okay, the translation was not perfect, but I understood. The next part was completely mangled, and I asked her clarifying questions. She'd gone to Oʻahu first and found out that Alice had been killed in an accident. "In Japan I studied a lawyer," the Google voice said. Must be Washburne. "I was cute to get answers."

The last part was so odd, and I figured out that Google had translated Kauaʻi as kawaii, or cute. Yumi had come to Kauaʻi to get answers.

Instead of meeting Washburne, she spoke to the ex-wife, Virginia. After that, she had all the information she needed to approach Court directly.

"I didn't think that I would do it this way." Google Translate was now completely unintelligible. From Yumi's expression, I knew she was revealing a hurt that was deeply personal. I wished I could follow exactly what she was confessing. "I was thinking only about my daughter. She was no longer my daughter."

She dissolved into tears, which dripped down her dark face onto the sand. I wasn't the huggy type, especially with people I didn't know too well, but I managed to pat her thin back.

I spoke into my phone. "Court knew nothing. And her parents, her adoptive parents, were scared to lose her." I didn't know the whole story behind the Lees' decisions, but they were good people, I told her.

Yumi shot me a side eye. She wasn't so sure.

"One thing I don't understand," I said. "Why were you in the ocean that Sunday?"

Yumi spread her arms out toward the ocean and explained how her home island was sinking into the sea. I knew enough about the Marshall Islands to follow her hand gestures. Someday in the not-too-distant future, her island would be completely submerged, just as Washburne himself had said. Nonetheless, the sea spoke to her, comforted her. She needed it to tell her the next step to get closer to her biological daughter.

She then spoke into my phone to explain what had happened next. She was in the water, up to her neck, when she felt herself being pulled down. She dog-paddled furiously, only to feel someone holding her from behind. "Go home to Japan," a man said. In both English and Japanese. And then she was dunked back in the water, where she struggled to breathe. She remembered nothing afterward.

I felt a current of fear go up my spine. Had it been the aging Washburne who had threatened her? But could he physically have done that? And what about speaking Japanese?

The wind was starting to whip through the bay, sending a salty coolness that made the hair on my legs stand on end. Grains of sand blew into our faces and clothing. I gestured that we should return to the car, and Yumi nodded. I put out my hand—the pandemic be damned—and her small freckled one grasped hold as I pulled her up.

When we reached the car, the cul-de-sac was almost deserted. Yellow crime tape was hung over the door of the Airbnb. Someone was leaning on the side of the Fiesta. Adam, his drone at his feet. My stomach got butterflies in spite of almost losing my life a mere hour ago. Maybe a relationship with this Adam Harjo did have potential.

"You didn't have to wait around for me," I said, but I was grateful that he was here now.

"How are you doing?"

I shook my head to indicate that it was too much for me to process right now. And then, to make sure he wouldn't think I was putting him off, I added, "I'll tell you everything later. Tonight, maybe? We can have drinks at Waimea Junction."

"How about an ice instead?"

Who would turn down an alcoholic drink for a shave ice? I was a bit flattered. Something from my past life was still desired.

"Is your drone okay?" I spoke of it almost like it was a living being.

"It's fine. But there's something I think you should see." He gestured toward a video on the screen of his phone.

I pulled out my mask from my pocket and put it on as I cozied up to Adam to watch the video. Yumi walked away to stare at the Airbnb, which was now officially closed to her.

"This is from Thursday morning by Alealea," Adam said, explaining that that was the morning Ted had been killed at Washburne's rental. A pickup truck pulled up to the house, and out came a figure in blue scrubs. That had to be Ted.

But wait a minute—he wasn't sneaking the back way, but walking straight up the front walkway, with a long, shiny item in his right hand. Most likely the machete.

"Can you zoom in to the man walking in the front yard?" I asked.

Adam poked at his phone and paused the image. The machete was completely identifiable. He pressed PLAY, and I continued watching. Ted walked to the front door, something blowing from his ear. The porch roof, unfortunately, shielded what happened next. The drone kept moving and circling over the area. When it returned to Washburne's rental, I spied not only a pickup truck parked on the street but also my turquoise Fiesta. Nothing more after that.

"I can't believe I have footage of the machete guy," Adam said.

"Machete guy" was apparently how Ted was being referenced in Kaua'i's social media circles.

"Well, it kinda proves that Washburne lied about how Ted got in," I said. "He said he broke in through the back window."

Adam didn't seem as enthused as I was. "You can't really clearly see where he went."

"Can you rewind to the place where he was walking in the front again?"

Adam did so and handed me the phone. When Ted was about halfway to the front door, I paused the video and pinched the image to enlarge it.

"Damn," I murmured.

"What?" Adam pulled his phone out of my hands and squinted at the blown-up image. "It looks like a black mask on the grass. Something with a pig on it." He shrugged his shoulders.

"That's no ordinary mask: that's an Arkansas Razorbacks mask."

The state university in Arkansas held no meaning for Adam, but it, in addition to the breaking of the glass *after* Ted was shot, could be the smoking gun for the case against Washburne. Andy's photo of the crime scene showed the mask inside the house. But how had it gotten inside if it had dropped from Ted's ear onto the front lawn? Obviously, somebody had placed it inside. And who else could it be but the shooter, Garvin Washburne, covering his tracks?

"Mahalo, Adam." I grasped hold of his elbow so tightly that he stepped away and mouthed an "ouch." If it hadn't been for COVID, I would have kissed him, so I had the pandemic to thank for restraining me.

"Please send that to me via Google docs or Dropbox or something."

"Will do. And I'll see you tonight."

I was glad my mask covered my grin, which probably was as big as the Joker's. I waved for Yumi to return to the car. She also had a rare smile on her face, revealing a crooked right eye tooth.

"Koibito?" she asked after Adam left with his drone.

Once we got inside, I opened Google Translate on my phone and motioned for her to repeat the word.

The female Google translated: "Lover."

I felt my face flush. "No, no. Not a lover." At least not yet. In the meantime, I got a Dropbox link from Adam. He did work fast. I forwarded it to Andy with a note about its contents. I thought this was definitive proof that Washburne was guilty, but who knew what the police would decide?

We remained quiet on the drive back to Waimea Junction. No Google Translate, no language miscommunications.

I pressed on Spotify, choosing my Beyoncé playlist. Yumi began beating her fingers on her thighs to the beat. Who would have thought that a middle-aged Marshallese woman who lived in Japan would be a Beyoncé fan?

The fourth song was the classic "Single Ladies." Yumi was trying her best with the lyrics, but when it came to the "oh oh oh," she was on it. Actually, both of us were. The car windows were down, and the ocean breeze was blowing our long hair out of its fasteners and bobby pins. "If you liked it, you should have put a ring on it! If you liked it, you should have put a ring on it!" Beyoncé crooned.

"Oh oh oh. Oh oh oh," we screamed, out of both tune and rhythm, but it didn't matter. We dissolved into much-needed laughter, not sure of what tomorrow would bring, but not caring, at least for the length of a song.

Once I pulled into the Waimea Junction parking lot, I saw that Lee's Leis and Flowers was open. The Lees' station wagon was out front. Mr. and Mrs. Lee must have heard from Court by now. I imagined they were overwhelmed with worry, but I knew the hospital wouldn't let them in to see their daughter. Damn COVID.

I removed my phone from its holder and returned to Google Translate. "Did you speak to Mrs. Lee about Court-*san?*" I asked.

Yumi listened carefully and then took the phone from my hands to read the written translation. She nodded.

That's all I needed to know. I sent Yumi over to Books and Suds with my extra key. I told her to take a rest on Sean's cot. In spite of our wild Beyoncé moment on the drive, I knew she was traumatized. I know I was.

"You hear about baby—"

"I'll tell you," I assured her.

She bowed slightly and made her way to Sean's former soap-and-used-book store.

I let out a big breath. Now to the Lees. I wasn't looking forward to talking with them. So awkward. I looked at them as my elders, especially the refined Mrs. Lee. To know of their deception was embarrassing. Baachan had her own childhood secrets, but I expected that. First, she was

super-old, and she was Baachan, uncouth and a bit filthy
at times. The Lees seemed so much more respectable, but
it turned out that they were as human as the rest of us in
Waimea.

I gathered my strength. Court was in a strange hospital
in Princeville, giving birth to a baby for the first time. If she
could go through that, I could poke and prod to discover
the full truth of how my best friend had come to Waimea.

I stood in the front doorway. Both the front and back
were wide open, and I smelled the sweet fragrance of freesia,
white ginger, and stephanotis.

They had received a new shipment of tropical flowers,
and I spotted Mr. Lee filling white plastic buckets with water
from an outside hose in the back. Mrs. Lee was perched at
the counter, trimming the ends of fresh flowers with a stem
cutter.

Her lined face brightened a little when she saw me.
"Have you heard anything yet?"

I shook my head and checked my phone to see if anything had come in about the birth during the last few seconds. Nothing.

I almost tiptoed—well, as much as I could in my
Crocs—into the flower shop as if there might be mine-
fields on the ground. I slumped onto one of the folding
chairs and adjusted one of the Lees' disposable masks over
my nose and face.

Mrs. Lee didn't hold her body like a woman expecting
to become a grandmother any moment. Her posture was
even more erect than usual. She assumed a defensive position, a wall that failed to reveal any cracks.

"You know some Japanese," I said. "I've heard you speak
to customers from Japan."

Mrs. Lee continued to trim her stems. *Snip. Snip. Snip.*

"I know you talked to Yumi Hara when she came by to pick up the lei."

"I suppose that makes me a bad person. A bad mother. That's what Court thinks, doesn't she?"

"She just doesn't understand. She wants to. I want to too."

Mrs. Lee stopped snipping her flower stems. She sat frozen, and for a moment I thought she might be having a stroke. Then the fissures in her composed stance appeared. She rocked back and forth in her seat and almost howled in pain.

Mr. Lee ran into the shop and his eyes darted between his crying wife and me.

"She's okay," I called out. "She's getting it all out."

He retreated back outside to tend to their cut blooms.

I let Mrs. Lee cry for a few minutes. In a way, I was thankful that we were in COVID times, which prevented me from scooping her up in my arms to both comfort her and make her stop crying. We all needed to break down sometimes. I felt all the pressures of these last several months loosen in my own body. Maybe when I was alone taking a bath tonight, my tears would come.

I handed her a box of tissues sitting in the middle of the table. She bobbed her head in thanks and pulled out a few, dabbing her eyes and fiercely blowing her nose.

"She told me she was looking for her daughter. A daughter she had given up when she was only twenty. She said she'd found out from someone in the attorney's office that we had adopted her. I was upset. That was confidential information. I told her to take her lei and leave. I had no idea she would have such an allergic reaction to the moki-hana berries."

More nose-blowing.

"The attorney's ex-wife showed Yumi the file. Washburne was the lawyer, right?"

Mrs. Lee nodded.

"Why didn't you tell Court that you'd gotten her through a private adoption?"

Mrs. Lee's mouth tightened in a straight line. It became more evident to me. "You found out that it was sketchy," I said.

Mr. Lee re-entered the room, wiping his hands on a rag. I got the feeling that he'd been listening the whole time.

"It was my decision as much as Chungmi's," he said. "That asshole lawyer contacted us when Court was around four to tell us that he was being investigated. And that we shouldn't come forward if we didn't want Court to be taken away from us."

"I'm not sure if we did the right thing," said Mrs. Lee, who had stopped crying. "I didn't want Court to be without us. We were all she knew."

It was a mess, and I knew the Lees adored Court. They had been a tad protective throughout her life. Maybe it was because they feared that Court being out in the world would mean that the truth would find her. And it had.

"I tried to put Court's birth mother out of my mind. But every Mother's Day, I couldn't help but think of her. The guilt made me sick."

Now that I thought of it, Mrs. Lee had always made sure that she was working on Mother's Day, the busiest time for the flower shop. After Court graduated from high school, she tried to make her mom take a break that day—at least work only part-time—but Mrs. Lee insisted that she needed to be at the shop full-force. I thought it was because

Court's mom was a workaholic, but the truth was that she wanted work as a distraction from her feelings.

"That day, my worst fears became real. She'd been a ghost before, and now she had a real face and body. I don't know why I spoke so harshly to her. I was trying to scare her away, pretend that she had no place in Court's life. And when I heard that she'd had a bad reaction to the mokihana, I realized that I'd forgotten to tell her to be careful, that some people have bad reactions where it touches your skin. Court is allergic to mokihana, so of course her birth mother would be too."

Mr. Lee was almost collapsed in the corner of the shop by the brooms and mop. He had no idea that his wife had actually spoken to Yumi before her incident at Waimea Bay.

"I'm sorry, Mike," she apologized to her husband. "I should have told you right away. Every day that I didn't say something just made it all the more worse. But I wanted her to be okay. Really, I did. I was in constant prayer for her recovery."

Mr. Lee pushed himself from the corner and went to his wife's side. "We have a second chance to make this all right."

We let Yumi rest in Books and Suds for another hour or so. Mrs. Lee made her a gorgeous bouquet of flowers, full of stephanotis and white ginger. It was all white, a symbol of truth and purity.

I was emotionally exhausted after all this truth-telling. But there was a loose end that needed to be tied up. Specifically, who had dunked Yumi in the water? Someone who had been close by and knew some basic Japanese. Someone who had arrived on the scene with wet hair to ironically save her. Rocket Nakayama.

He was right in front of the hospital, sitting on the stoop and sucking his vape as if he'd sensed that I was on

my way. He registered no emotion as I parked and got out
of the Fiesta.

"Don't start on me, Leilani. I know."

"What do you know?"

"Court told her madda, who told your baachan, who
told my madda."

"What?" As Baachan had been sequestered at home, she
was now often on our landline, talking story with members
of her ukulele group and old friends. She'd managed to get
the word out a lot faster than I could.

"I know who dat lady Yumi is. Court's real madda."
Rocket looked miserable. For all his faults, he valued mothers probably more than anything else in his life. "Washburne
told me to scare her. Not hurt her. You believe me, eh?"

As far as I knew, Rocket had never been a threat to
anyone beside himself.

"And you were following me dat one day from Lydgate."

Rocket swallowed before speaking. "I lost control of
Taiji's bike. Wasn't trying to run you over."

Yeah, Taiji's motorcycle was definitely junk.

"I told Washburne I couldn't keep following you. He
got me out of trouble a few years back, but you a friend from
small-kid time. Can't cross dat line."

Rocket had his own code of honor, which didn't apply
to outsiders like Yumi.

"You know you'll have to go to the police."

Rocket nodded. "Already called Andy. He's on his way."

I had so many questions—like, why did he do it? Did
Washburne have anything on him? If he revealed all to the
authorities, I hoped it would buy him some goodwill.

I checked my phone to see if Kelly had texted me. No
news yet. "Well, I betta go. Take care, Rocket."

He nodded his head and put down his vape.

When I returned to Waimea Junction, Sophie was the only one seated on the bench in front of the picnic table by the parking lot. I parked; when I joined her at the table, she leapt up as if I was infected with something even more undesirable than the virus.

"Sophie, sit down. Please."

Sophie reluctantly did as I asked.

"I'm really sorry about Ro," I said, pulling my body up so I faced her squarely.

Sophie turned her head away.

"And you're right. I wasn't thinking about how important she is to you. You two have been friends since elementary school. Court and I have known each other since middle school. Way later."

Sophie's jaw lost some of its tightness. I was reaching her.

"I have an idea for how to get Ro back in Waimea."

"We can foster?" Sophie finally looked at me. Her eyes were red, probably from lack of sleep.

I shook my head. "We can't. But maybe someone else can."

Before I could elaborate, about half a dozen teenagers flooded into Waimea Junction. We had to move another picnic table next to the two other ones out front. Some smarter students had showed up to help tutor the ones who were struggling.

We were moving the picnic tables so the sun wouldn't hit their laptop screens full-on when a familiar white SUV pulled into our parking lot. I could barely see the taxi driver, Mama Liu, over the steering wheel. My father and Sean popped out from the back seat and waved from a distance.

"Turns out we were on the same flight from Oʻahu," Sean called out. He was wearing a Killer Wave mask, while my father had his dangling from one ear. Dad said nothing, but, based on the rare smile on his face, I knew he'd managed to forge some kind of deal for his mask enterprise.

Normally Sophie would have run to greet Dad. But she was too absorbed in talking to a boy across the table from her. She was growing up.

"Got to quarantine now for three days before we get tested," Sean said through his mask. "Your dad will be staying with me to make sure you'll all be safe."

Sean with Dad? That was the strangest combination. I was sure they weren't heading for a bromance; but for Dad to have even agreed was a miracle in itself.

"Let's Facetime tonight," I called out. "I have a proposal for you."

Sean nodded. "It certainly looks like you've been busy."

"Go by the house," I told Dad. "Just to at least wave to Mom."

He gave me a shaka sign in affirmation.

I went back into Santiago's to rearrange items in the refrigerator and our shelves. Having regular giveaways required a lot of maintenance: checking on expired items and throwing them away, making sure that the same products were grouped together. Since we had received a lot of toiletries from Sean's contact, I was thinking of bagging mini-toothpastes, soaps, razors, and sanitary napkins and distributing them to the homeless encampment at Salt Pond.

I was pulling out some plastic bags when my phone buzzed. Court? No, it was Taylor on Facetime. Oops. She was probably peeved that I hadn't given her any updates about the incident at the Airbnb.

"Ah, hello."

"Why didn't you call me?"

"I've been kinda busy." *Foiled a kidnapping and potential murder (mine) shortly before my BFF started going into labor. Not everything is about you, Taylor.*

"The chief just had his press conference outside the station. He said you were the one who intervened in Yumi Hara's abduction."

"Yeah, I can't get into it much right now. Have to go in to the station soon to make some official statements."

"C'mon, you can give me at least a little something."

"Why should I?"

"I can trade you some information. I found Ted's people in the Ozarks in Arkansas."

"The Ozarks?" That sounded like hillbilly country.

"A town called Springdale." Taylor went on to explain that about 15,000 Marshallese people live in Arkansas, the second-largest population of the islanders after Hawai'i. I was amazed.

"Why Arkansas?" I asked.

"A lot of them work in poultry factories there. It all started with a Marshallese graduate of the University of Oklahoma finding a job in that industry. The news spread to other people on the islands. Adoption attorneys then got involved in getting Marshallese babies adopted in Arkansas."

"That is so weird," I said.

"Not totally weird. I mean, you have the Hmong in Minnesota, Cambodians in California. It happens."

"But at least California is next to the Pacific Ocean."

Taylor pursed her lips.

"So, what about Ted?"

"His sister died of COVID early on. In May. While she was hospitalized, he apparently got a call from a woman

who worked with Washburne. About how the sister might
have been illegally taken from her birth mother."

"Shit."

"I know, right? I spoke to one of his friends, another
nurse, who said he was enraged to hear about this. After she
died, he didn't know what to do. He knew that Washburne
was in Kaua'i somewhere and went on a hunt for him."

"What, to avenge the trafficking of his adopted sister?"

"Something like that. Who knows? This pandemic has
hit people in different ways."

"You have a photo of his sister?"

"I do. Why?"

"Can you send it to me?"

"You can't give it to any media outlets."

"I'm not, okay? Just for personal use."

"Okay." Taylor was not enthused, but I knew she'd follow through. One thing about Taylor, she was a woman of
her word. "So, what about what happened at the Airbnb?"

I told her the whole story, leaving out Adam and the
drone. I didn't want to drag him into something he might
not want. I wasn't sure why I was being so protective of him,
but he had done me a great favor, beyond the call of duty.

Taylor was lapping up these tidbits like a feral cat drinks
milk. I didn't care what she posted on her news website. It
did have the power to damage people's reputations, and if her
story maligned Garvin Washburne I was in full support of it.

A few minutes after we ended our Facetime session, my
phone dinged again. Taylor had texted the photo of Ted's
sister. She was small-boned like a Marshallese woman, with
long wavy hair and a shy smile. She must have been in her
twenties, like Court. Too young. I thought COVID only cut
down the lives of seniors.

We had an old color printer in the shack, and some of the ink had dried out. I borrowed Dani's laptop from school, downloaded the photo, and printed it out in black and white. Not great, but it would have to do. I taped the photo in a corner of the shack. I went next door to Lee's and picked up a handful of mokihana berries that were starting to lose their shape and arranged them with some of the greens. That would be my floral arrangement in memory of both Ted and Ted's sister.

I sat alone in the dark for a while, thinking about all the losses we'd suffered these past few months. Yet the Santiagos were still intact. That's what mattered most. And maybe we could help others stay intact like us. I heard cheers outside and went to see what the excitement was all about. Mrs. Lee had brought out plates full of cut watermelon wedges for the teens. She offered a slice first to one of the younger kids, who shyly accepted. Even though she'd hid the adoption details, Mrs. Lee had been a good mother to Court, raising her with a firm but gentle hand.

The plates were emptied in seconds—these kids were eating monsters. Watching this confirmed for me how Court's empty childhood bedroom could change someone's life.

"Mrs. Lee, do you really believe in second chances?" I asked, taking the plates wet with watermelon juice from her.

She glanced at me with a little confusion as we walked inside the flower shop.

In a hushed voice, I explained Ro's situation. How she was a good kid who needed a safe place to land. And a room of her own.

The Lees could certainly provide safety, and they had an extra room. They'd been thinking of converting it into a nursery for when they'd babysit their future grandchild, but what did an infant need? Dry diapers, milk, and love. The three essentials. Simple. Uncomplicated.

"If it's okay with Mike, she can stay with us," Mrs. Lee said. And we both knew that if it was okay with her, it would be fine with her husband.

I didn't want to say anything to Sophie, not until we had more confirmation from DCFS. But I was hopeful.

Emily walked into Lee's during all this madness. "Dad told me you were here. You've ruined my quiet study area with all these kids." She said it with smiling eyes, so I knew she wasn't mad. She then told me, "I need to borrow the car."

"Pekelo?" I asked.

"We want to go out for a celebratory drink. Andy called him and told him that his story completely checked out. And the foundation emailed me to say that my scholarship has been restored. They said there was some kind of mix-up."

Yeah, I figured. And I was sure the mix-up involved Garvin Washburne. "So did Andy say anything about Washburne?"

Emily shook her head. "But my friend in the DA's office said they're preparing to charge him with either second-degree murder or manslaughter, in addition to kidnapping Yumi. They found evidence that he let Ted Rumpf into the house through the front door and then killed him inside. Garvin lied about Ted breaking in through the back window. The glass shards should have been inside the house, not outside. Plus, Ted's mask was on the front lawn. Garvin found it and planted it inside as well. Why go to all that trouble if he wasn't trying to cover his tracks?"

I wanted to interrupt and say *Yeah, I found the evidence about the mask.* But for what purpose? Just so I got some credit? As long as Washburne was held accountable for what he'd done, that's all I cared about. And that my sister could continue her legal studies on the Mainland.

"Em, I'm so happy for you." I refrained from giving her a big hug.

"Depending on how COVID goes, I might be able to go back to Santa Clara in the spring. Pekelo is thinking of coming with me. He worked with computers in the Navy. There may be something for him in Silicon Valley."

I narrowed my eyes. I'd never heard Pekelo talk about anything related to high tech. But I knew he was desperate to get out of Hawai'i and seek his fortune on the Mainland. I wasn't sure if Silicon Valley was ready for a tatted native Hawaiian, but maybe someone there would welcome him with open arms.

I was feeling generous, so I went into Santiago's, put on some sheer plastic gloves, and pulled out an ice mold I'd stuck in the freezer. I guided it through our machine, which spit out the most beautiful fine shave ice. I wasn't ready to give this business up yet. But maybe I'd have to pivot slightly. I knew all about pivoting from my PE classes. Keep one foot glued to the ground while the other darts in different directions. I was committed to Kaua'i and Santiago's, but maybe I had to experiment more with the services we offered. Seeing the teens congregating at the shack made me think. I could form a nonprofit to help at-risk kids with their studies. A portion of our shave ice profits could help fund some of the expenses. Of course, I'd have to make sure we actually *had* profits, not to mention make enough to pay me a salary, but with Sean's help maybe I could make it happen.

"Waimea Wonder," a familiar gruff voice called through our open service window.

"Baachan, you can't be here. Not safe."

"Can't stay inside forever."

I sympathized with her. "Well, at least wear a mask." I handed her a blue disposable one. Under protest, she fastened the loops around her droopy earlobes, lowering the mask under her nose.

"Sit in the car and wait. Too many keiki running around." Waimea Junction had become kid central; I'm sure germs were left on all surfaces of the shack.

Baachan trudged toward the Ford. I kept my eye on her until she got into the driver's seat.

I made Baachan's ice first. I piled on the azuki beans, her favorite. She deserved a special treat.

Like a drive-through waitress, I brought Baachan the ice that she'd invented up to the car window. She couldn't roll down the window without the car keys and so opened the door to accept the ice.

"Mahalo," she uncharacteristically said to thank me.

"Enjoy but don't spill, yah?"

I was on my way to pick up more ices when my phone vibrated in my pocket and I paused to read a group text from Kelly.

"It's a girl!" I shouted.

Baachan was midway through a bite, her upper denture falling slightly.

I returned to the car window. "Court had a girl!"

Big crooked smile.

I Facetimed Kelly, and instead of his face I saw Court's sweat-soaked one, her hair back in a blue paper cap and a mask over her mouth. In her arms was a naked, squirmy baby.

I yelped again. Yup, I was going to be one of *those* aunties.

"Do you want to know her name?" Court asked me.

The egomaniac in me prepared to hear "Leilani."

Instead, Court said, "Mokihana Chungmi Kahuakai."

I silently absorbed the name. Mokihana for how she was reunited with her birth mother and, of course, to honor Kaua'i. And Chungmi after her adoptive mother. It certainly covered all the bases.

"What do you think?"

"Perfect," I said. "It's absolutely perfect."

By this time, Yumi had awakened from her nap inside Books and Suds. She carried the floral bouquet in the crux of her arm like she was Mrs. America.

"Yumi-*san*," I called out. "Court had her baby! Girl."

"*Girlru*," she repeated, a dreamy smile on her face. Mrs. Lee took a few steps toward Yumi and then one step back. She continued this odd dance until they were face-to-face. Mrs. Lee examined Yumi's face as if she was seeing which features were the same as Court's.

"*Omedetou*," she said to Yumi.

Yumi bowed slightly. "Con-gratu-lations."

The sight of the two mothers making peace was making me teary-eyed. Mr. Lee, leaning against the front of Lee's Leis and Flowers, was actively bawling, giving me permission to be Ms. Waterworks too. Now was the time to cry.

The teens, picking up on the emotions of the adults, were getting out of control. Their Google Meet class had ended, and they were huddling together, doubled over in laughter over whatever TikTok videos they were watching on their phones.

"Hold up, everyone! Take care of laptops and put in a safe place. And wear your masks!"

No one—even the adults—was listening to me on that last part. Baachan had escaped the Fiesta and sat in a beach chair that she'd found in Killer Wave. She was unmasked too, but at least she was socially distanced.

A tiny Smart car rolled into the parking lot. A familiar figure emerged from the driver's seat, only instead of in a man bun, his long hair was loose, almost down to his waist. And per Mayor Kawakami's order, he was wearing a mask.

"Hi," he said to me.

"Oh, hi."

"I came for my shave ice."

"You got it."

Out of the corner of my eye, I saw Yumi mouthing the new Japanese word I'd learned today. *Koibito*. It was much too early for that, but I wouldn't mind getting my fingers tangled in that long, beautiful hair.

Adam followed me into Santiago's as I finished making shave ice for everyone. I even got some sake and rum from D-man's bar to supplement the shave ice for the adults.

Adam helped me distribute the ices to Sophie, her friends, and the Lee clan, which now included Yumi.

"Cheers!" Mr. Lee called out.

"Kanpai!" Yumi said joyfully in her best Beyoncé holler.

"Kāmau!" we all said in unison.

THE END

To support efforts to reduce food insecurity in Kauaʻi, consider donating to the 501(c)3 nonprofit Hawaiʻi Foodbank Kauaʻi: https://hawaiifoodbank.org/Kauaʻi-donate

#RiseResiliently

Checks made out to Foodbank Kauaʻi can be mailed to P.O. Box 1671, Līhuʻe, HI 96766.

Pidgin (Hawaiian Creole) and Location Names

I'm not from Hawai'i, but I have been influenced by and exposed to the culture through my life here in California as well as occasional visits to the Islands. From my college days to working at *The Rafu Shimpo* newspaper, I could not help but to be touched by the people and food of Hawai'i.

While I've read many books written in pidgin, I certainly am no expert on this dialect. I've used it sparingly to give the story some authentic flavor. Cynthia Hughes of Honolulu has been a godsend and careful reader and corrector of the pidgin in this mystery. All errors are mine.

In terms of location names like Hawai'i and Kaua'i, I've chosen to use the okina, which is often mistaken for an apostrophe. The okina is a glottal stop in Polynesian languages such as Hawaiian. The University of Hawai'i explains that the okina is "similar to the sound between the syllables of 'oh-oh.'" To respect the origins of the Islands, I've chosen to adopt the use of the okina in names of places and people. The same goes with the kahako, or macron, which indicates the elongation of a vowel sound. I've eliminated both when used in a proper name such as Lihue Airport or Kauai Community Correctional Facility.

I've eliminated any italicization of pidgin or Asian-language words commonly used in Hawai'i. However, more unusual words not used in common speech have been italicized.

Select Pidgin, Hawaiian, and Japanese Words
(not a complete list)

'āina (Hawaiian): land

aisus: shucks, darn it (spoken by Filipinos)

'amakiji: Hawaiian bird

baachan (Japanese): grandma

baka or bakatare (Japanese): stupid

broke da mouth: delicious

chawan (Japanese): rice bowl

chicken skin: goosebumps

dem: them or others

furikake (Japanese): dry Japanese seasoning, usually with bits of nori

gambatte (Japanese): hang in there

gohan (Japanese): rice

grindz: food

hammajang: mess

haole (Hawaiian): white person, non-Hawaiian

hashi (Japanese): chopsticks

huhu (Hawaiian): angry, mad

kalo (Hawaiian): taro

kama'āina (Hawaiian): resident of the Islands

kāmau (Hawaiian): persevere, to your health

kānaka maoli (Hawaiian): Native Hawaiian

kanpai (Japanese): cheers

kawaii (Japanese): cute

kine: kind

koibito (Japanese): lover

lilikoi (Hawaiian): passionfruit

lolo (Hawaiian): crazy

mahalo (Hawaiian): thank you

mento: mental, crazy, silly

mu'umu'u (Hawaiian): long, flowy dress

musubi (Japanese): rice ball

niele (Hawaiian): nosy, curious

obake (Japanese): ghost

ofuro (Japanese): tub

okole (Hawaiian): butt

'ohana (Hawaiian): family

omedetou (Japanese): congratulations

one: a or the

one oddah: another

onolicious: delicious

'ōpū (Hawaiian): belly

pilau (Hawaiian): spoiled, rotten

rubbah slippahs: flip-flops

shaka: hang loose hand sign

shamoji (Japanese): paddle to scoop rice

shibai: drama or lies

shinpai (Japanese): worry

shi-shi (Japanese): pee

shōganai (Japanese): it can't be helped

slippah: sandals (slippers)

small-kid time: childhood, back in the day

sōka (Japanese): that's right

somen (Japanese): thin noodles
stink eye: dirty looks
talk stink: talk bad about someone
tamago (Japanese): egg
tutu (Hawaiian): grandmother
uji: gross
ujikintoki (Japanese): combination of tea and red bean
utsukushii (Japanese): beautiful
wahine: girl
wen: used to express past tense

About the Author

Naomi Hirahara is an Edgar Award-winning author of multiple traditional mystery series and noir short stories. Her *Mas Arai* mysteries, which have been published in Japanese, Korean, and French, feature a Los Angeles gardener and Hiroshima survivor who solves crimes. Her first historical mystery is *Clark and Division*, which follows a Japanese American family's move to Chicago in 1944 after being released from a California wartime detention center. A former journalist with *The Rafu Shimpo* newspaper, Naomi has also written numerous nonfiction history books and curated exhibitions. She has also written two middle-grade books, the novel *1001 Cranes*, and the upcoming nonfiction anthology, *We Are Here: 30 Inspiring Asian Americans and Pacific Islanders Who Have Shaped the United States*.